ONCE THE BIRDS FLY

A Novel

HUMA ADNAN

To Adnan,
my life.
Sam,
my light
&
the birds which flew
away.

PART ONE

FAIZ

One

I am going to see her after twenty-five years. Twenty-five long years. The figure is too small, but it has many microseconds, minutes and days dissolved in it. What had happened during these days, I don't know. Whether she remembers me or not, even that, I don't know.

I still remember the first time I met her. She was warm, friendly and serious. She was like the sound of that jet that I fly everyday, which bangs in the sky but disappears in another second. She always told me to be a writer, but I was too stubborn to take any advice. Perhaps, all those articles I wrote were either to impress her or to take good grades. I don't know. But what am I doing today? Am I curious to know whether she missed me all this time or do I really care about her? Whatever is the reason, all I know is I just want to see her.

They told me that she said she has something to tell me or (I think) give me. I didn't force to know, as I know she would have asked not to tell. She is good in keeping suspense. She is that treasure trunk which has been recovered after thousands of years, but can never be opened as the key has been lost. Do I have the key? No!

I remember my friends interrogating me about whom did I message a lot and I would just smile. Did she really matter to me? I think... no! Yes! No! I don't know. How can I? No it's not possible. It was not possible. All these years I had been so much busy with traveling, family and kids that I really forgot her and suddenly two days ago I got the call from her home saying I should see her as it's urgent. When I asked why she didn't call by herself, the man on the phone said she was busy and asked him to pass the message. It's the first time in my life I planned a trip without thinking for once. I didn't even ask my wife or said anything at work. I packed my luggage and took the first flight to Islamabad. After reaching there, I have to take a drive to Murree, a hilly area in the north where I have never been before.

While I was packing my luggage my wife asked why I was in such a hurry. Why was I dropping things. "Why are you panicked?"

"No. I am not."

"Nervous?"

"Hell, no!"

She looked at me gravely and then smiled. "You will never admit that, will you?"

I decided to stay quiet.

I remember that, when I was asked to join the reunion of aviators and, most important to present the person behind my success, I went into nostalgia. My wife must have expected it was herself, who has been my strength. Of course she is, but she doesn't share the part when I was a fledgling bird. When I was not a successful pilot. When I was an ordinary high school student. When I got the invitation I wished for the first time in life that *she* was there or at least, that I had any contact with her. If my mother hadn't been in India, then I would surely have taken her. It is good she wasn't there then. I cannot bear the mother-in-law's and daughter-in-law's silent conflict. This is a modern era where man is on verge of making time travel true. Everything has changed except this universal relation.

It took me almost eight hours to travel by plane. Now it would take another two hours to reach her home. I hate long drives. I don't know why the ones who fly high are so scared of grounds. Does it happen to eagles, falcons and vultures, also? What am I? Human, bird or alien? I remember her calling me alien. In those days I had a weird hair style. It was neither straight, nor flat. Girls would die on it; they used to call me "Mr. Charming", which was quiet flattering, and I enjoyed it.

Whenever I would tell her about my fights in school, unlike my Mom she never scolded me. All she said… no, she never said anything, she only smiled. Yes, she only smiled. Did she ever listen? Or did she never bother? Of course she least cared about it. She had so much to bother about. But what was that? Who knows? Maybe I will find the answers tonight.

"Why are you driving so fast?" I inquire from the driver.

"Sahib, this isn't safe time. There are lots of thieves. If I drove slowly, they would take this car and cook us for their meal."

"Are they cannibals??" I reply, shocked.

"*Han jee*! My mother used to say soon there would come a time when a human would eat another human's flesh. See, Sahib, this is the time!! You know in my neighborhood a lady ate her kids and gave the same meal to her husband. Now both of them are admitted to mental hospital. And on another day…"

"How long will it take??" I shiver and interrupt.

"Sahib jee, with this speed I will take you there in an hour."

"Hmm..." I nod."Are you going to see someone special?" He questions again.

"What?? Hmm. Ya. Ya....yes she..is.. someone.. yes, relative.. special."

I wonder why I mumbled. It was the first time I called her *my* relative. I never understood why I couldn't introduce her or talk about her with any of my friends or especially my wife.

Drivers have exhausting jobs and to overcome this tiredness they talk. They talk as much as they can. You could compile one book in a day, if you happened to travel in a cab all day. They have numberless stories, told and untold. Some of which they heard from their fellows, and some, they have created by reading the minds of their clients. There's no harm in listening these magnificent tales. As soon as I will leave the vehicle, my time to be a legend would start. I wonder what this driver would tell to his next client about me or my mumbling on his succinct question.

All these years I thought we can get the chance to get lost from the world, but how insane I was to think that's so. How can we get lost, if we are running in a circle? The circle will end and we will reach the same point from where we started our escape. She always used to say that a man can run as fast as cheetah, but he would never be able to escape from this world. Wild life has nothing to escape from; it is us, humans, who are civilized creatures, who possess the desire for escape.

"Jee sir, we have reached. Do you know the street?"

It takes me 15 seconds to come back from my space of imagination. I can't understand what he asked. I ask him, like a scared child, to repeat his question.

"We are in Eden Colony's phase 2. What is the street number?"

I take the paper from my wallet with trembling hands.

"Uumm f-five, five is the street number. House B20."

As soon as I see the house I get butterflies in stomach. After long time I am feeling so confused and panicked. It reminds me of my school days when before every exam I had cramps in my stomach and my hands would become cold and sweaty. I slowly take my luggage and pay the driver the demanded money, as there is no trend of calculating fares using meter. Although I know he asked me quite an extra amount I still ask him to keep the change. I am either in hurry or in anxiety to ring the bell of the door. In these five minutes I have brushed my hair with my fingers almost ten times. I hear somebody's footsteps approaching the door. My lips stretch and I don't know why I am smiling. In front of me there is a fourteen feet black iron driveway gate. Slowly, somebody unlocks it, and an old man with the age of 55 or 58 is standing in front of me. His hair is white and grey and he has a long white beard on his face. He is wearing Shalwar Kameez and neither smiles nor frowns. He politely asks me, "Are you Faiz?" The stretched smile has already disappeared and I just nod

I follow the old man into the house. He opens the door and announces loudly as if it was my surprised visit, "*Baaji*! Faiz sahib is here!" *Baaji*?? The word strikes me and takes me many years back. It is so new and fresh, as it had been just lost in the air and was waiting for me. As soon I entered, this word has circled me and I've started smiling innocently like in the hope that I would return it back to the owner. I wonder, has she gotten so old that this man is calling her *Baaji* or did she choose to be called *Baaji,* after I left? Heart in heart I smile and wonder whether I am still known among her acquaintances. Of course I must be! She promised me twenty-five years ago she would never forget me.

PARI

Two

Storytelling is a strange creation; it soothes us and sometimes plays skillfully with our emotions. It slowly rips up the delicate cores of our heart that no one has ever touched. For an instant we forget that we are enjoying the reflection of our own self in the dancing phonemes of the story, the image that we hide from our souls. By climbing each part of a story we whisper, yes, it is me. Oh, yes, it is so me! The question is, do we open up the hidden ourselves or do we burry it deep down the turning pages? Everyone in this world has an untold story in their heart. It's a story that is neither shared nor recalled in one's mind. The reasons are obvious: it can either be rejected by society or it gives too much pain to recall. Whatever the reason is, all I know is that my story is now no more 'untold'. A story of love with stories of love.

It is hard to push back the one you love. It takes your whole heart and soul. Sometimes, it takes that part of us and we move around like a body with no head or with a big hole in the chest. It's great that people can't see this image of ours that we hide inside. If they would, there would certainly be screams of people going mad out of fear. I pushed someone back, too. I pushed that person away from me and my life. It wasn't that I never loved that person, but I let him go because he mattered more than he should have.

Love is strange. It isn't something that can be defined. It has no mass and body. It is impossible to fit it in a jar or a box. If something can't fit, how can you define it? A pity is that love has always been defined as a relation between a man and woman. A love which is made in bed. A love whose motive has always been marriage. What we forget to notice is the love which lives inside us without any form, quantity or contract: it's a kind of love whose motive isn't marriage, but rather the construction of the beloved. I too always wondered whether such love exists. Is it possible that love has any other motive than to make love and produce offspring? After having a thousand years of learning in my short countable lifespan, I found or rather *discovered* that it does exist. It's only that we are too blind to feel it. We are coward to appreciate such unnoticed love, as we consider it minor. We think that it's unnecessary and that appreciating such love is needless. While we forget that love needs to be watered. It needs sunlight. It needs a constant reminder to grow and flourish and to breathe in new life every day.

This story is no different from other stories. It has tales within tales. It is made of strands of fables. But, like all the stories, it has the heart involved in it. A few people became so much important to me that I lost the importance in each and everything existing in the world. I made many people my Qibla and would revolve around them 24-7. But this story doesn't start here. It happened years ago. It happened when I lost the meaning in life.

Three

Memories never die. For me they never did. I can recall the first memory of three years old *me* sitting in a gallery. My heart was thumping inside my chest (like it usually happened when my Ama woke me up for school). But that moment, I was not going to school as it was evening and schools were closed and I wished I actually was in school.

My name is Pari: it's a strange name for many people. Ama told me that she named me Pari after her best friend. After school she lost all her contacts with her friends, so to keep her memories alive she named me Pari. My class teacher Miss Naila told us once that Pari is a lucky fairy and she flies really high. If she ever sits on someone's shoulder, then that person will become the Ruler of the country. Since then my classmates teased me and said, "Pari come and sit on us", and I really didn't mind that. Once, while cutting onions, Ama also asked me, Pari why don't you sit on me? I was surprised to hear that. When I stared at her face I saw tears were rolling down her cheeks. On my inquiry she said it was because of onions but I thought she wanted to be a ruler. I didn't understand back then why she wanted that, because she was a rich woman although she never dressed like rich ladies. She was always simple and would hardly put any makeup on. I think she did not like that, even though she had one old red lipstick in her drawer. Sometimes I would secretly use that for my doll, and I would think, *When I grow up I will always put lipstick like Miss Naila. She is beautiful, I wish I can go to her house and play with her. I feel so lucky when she lets me sit on her lap when our driver is late to pick me from school.* Those were times I wished that I would never go back home but then I used to worry about Ama. I couldn't even think of leaving her because I, as a child, thought she needed me always and she couldn't see me going.

In one of the typical evenings at home, the noise in Ama's bedroom started to increase. I was scared. I didn't know how long I hid there in the balcony, but I couldn't even go to her room, as I knew the door was locked from inside. I had to wait until he left. Something hit the wooden door; I could hear the bang, "was it a chair or Ama?" I hoped he was not beating her. Ama would always say he was a good man because he loved cats. Many times I saw him feeding cats. I was sure he loved Ama too. What he was saying? I couldn't understand the meaning of those words but I couldn't even hear Ama. Aba was always loud while Ama never spoke out or interrupted. She used to say when elders are speaking we shouldn't interrupt them; it is a sign of disrespect. Maybe he was older than her: that is why she never interrupted.

"I am going to burn you! Do you understand?

"What you brought with you when you married me? Just one suit? You should thank me I have given you this palace to live."

There was another smashing sound inside the room.

"You are sucking my blood! You are my maid! So do not ask me again why I come late! Understood?"

While roaring like a loin and slamming all the doors behind him, he left the house. I climbed down from a gallery entered into my room. I made sure that he had already gone after carefully witnessing from window. I crossed the living room and went up to her room. She was not there and I sat on the corner of the bed so I tried not to wrinkle the tidily spread bed sheet. I was sure she was hurt and had some wounds. I thought I would kiss her on her cheek and everything would have been alright.

"Ama!" I ran and hugged her.

But she wasn't crying. Her face was peaceful. She was smiling like Miss Naila, so I thought Aba didn't hit her. I saw no wounds and I was satisfied. But in the coming years I had to learn that wounds aren't always visible. They are untouchable like a soul inside the body whose existence is even doubted by many. Ama was right in saying that Aba was the best. I believed her when she said the he was the best father in the whole world and my world's name was Quetta.

Four

Quetta: a small valley with spectacular mountains, mellifluous fountains and eye-catching gardens. This is the place where I was destined to born. Geographically this small valley is surrounded by three craggy mountains. It is definitely a fruit-basket place. From plums to apples and from pomegranates to cherries, all adds up beauty to this fairy-tale land. Geologists say that once this valley was a sea. After millions years, the water dried off leaving behind this land, where later people settled for bread and shelter.

There are myths too. There's one huge mountain which can be seen from any part of the valley. This isn't a mountain; it is a complete figure of a sleeping woman, similar to Disney's Sleeping Beauty. There are number of stories regarding this mountain. Some say, there was a shepherd who was deprived of children. One day a beggar came to his door and asked for some bread. The kind wife of the shepherd gave him all the food that was in the house and in return she asked him to pray that she may have a son. The poor beggar gave her seven sugar lumps and asked her to eat only one and save the other six for the future, as each lump would give her one boy, and the poor man left. The lady, who had been patient for so many years, either couldn't believe the man or was too curious to know the results, so she ate all the seven lumps of sugar. Miracles happen when we least expect them: soon she bore seven healthy beautiful boys, but was physically too unfit to survive. So she quietly cuddled the death, leaving behind all she ever desired. Some say that her face turned into snow: that's why it snows heavily on that particular mountain up till now, while other tell that she became so gorgeous at the time of her death that her husband lost his senses and left the boys on their own and disappeared.

I believe more in the mythical part. Maybe it's because stories fascinate me. Every night, before going to sleep, Ama used to tell me a story. As soon as the story ended, she would hand over me to darkness and disappear into her dark room that she was ought to share with him. I know she didn't like being there. I would tell myself, *She needs me, as she loves me, and of course she wants me to be with her. One day, when I'll grow up, I'll bring her out of that dark room. Like a prince of a story I will free her. She is my princess and I will build a castle for her where only the two of us are going to live.*

We lived in the center of the town. It wasn't a crowded town like many capital cities, but it wasn't peaceful, in center. In the early morning the town would echo with the sound of rickshaws, motor bikes, cars and of hawkers shouting loudly to sell goods. Dad loved being there, as he said in case of emergency we could easily reach a dispensary or, if there was some more serious problem, we might quickly rush to the hospital. I didn't understand, who would be rushed to the hospital. I think Ama would. She often visited the hospital, at least five times in a month and sometimes she stayed there too. I didn't like to visit her in the hospital and see her with some strange pipes all around her. They put some straws in her nose and asked her to sleep. One of the nurse once said to me that I was not taking care of Ama. How could she say that? In fact, I was the only one who loved her in that house. Did the nurse tell the same thing to Aba? I think she should have. Before leaving the house to visit her in the hospital I would often convince myself, "No, I am not going to see her." I would pray and ask God not to send Ama again to the hospital. It hurt her and it hurt me more. I wish she always stayed here in that house which was near to the park, the bakery and the ice cream shop.

On our right lived Uncle Farid. I couldn't call him Farid or Mr. Farid, Ama said it was rude and only bad kids call elders by name. Next to uncle Farid's was my friend Saba's house. She and I were in the same school. In fact, all of her sisters were, but we didn't go together. Aba didn't like that I talked to them, but what he didn't know is I often visited them on special holidays. One day, before leaving the house on Eid, Ama said, "Don't tell Aba that you went to Saba's home, else he would lock the door for ever and you will never step out of the house anymore."

"Jee Ama," I sheepishly replied.

There were three houses on one side of our street and on the opposite of ours lived Tipu Bhai. I don't know why he was called Tipu but he was my brother's friend. He often took me to his home and I played with him. I didn't like his Ama as she never smiled like my Ama. Next to Tipu lived Khala Samrina. No one would see her much often. She only came out if she had to complain about someone.

I never liked to stay too long in my house: it wasn't that my house was small, but there wasn't much there, to stay for. Both the roars and the graveyard-like silence always made me wish to stay away, to roam on the roads and never step inside those tall walls. I had two half-sisters, Salma and Sobia, three half-brothers Elias, Taha and Taimoor, and my only brother from Ama was Furqaan. Salma was the eldest, who was married before I was born and lived in Sibi after her marriage, with her husband, two sons and a daughter. Her eldest son was of my age. He often teased me and called me *Khala (aunt)*. After Salma was Elias, the most beloved of Aba. He generously spent Aba's money on alcohol. Aba and Elias were aware of each other's secrets, but each one always pretended not to know which pleasures the other was pursuing. Elias was married to Asma and, with both her and his son, he lived with us. After Elias came Taha, who married a German lady and settled in Germany with one son and two girls. Right after one year Taha was followed by Taimoor, who lived close to us with one daughter and a son. He left the house after my birth, but I hardly have any memory of that separation. Aba often mentioned that Taimoor filed the case against him and asked for the share in property, and that, to maintain his reputation and not to drag the case in court, Aba gave him in a large sum of money and asked him to leave the house. Taimoor never asked Aba to give him a place in the house and never even showed any regret after spending the rest of his life in one bedroom, a small hall and an open air kitchen and a toilet which was covered with a thick plastic sheet throughout the year. Sobia followed Taimoor after ten years. People would often be surprised by how there was no production of offspring during these years; what they never knew is that Aba's first wife gave birth to three lifeless babies during these ten years. When Sobia was only two, Aba's first wife left the world of men with her ninth baby during labor. Maybe God thought to free her from the trialed life and to start the test of my Ama. When Aba's first wife, who was a sister of my Ama, died Salma was 17, Elias 15, Taha 13, Taimoor 12, and Sobia only 2 years old. At the time of her death, Aba's first wife, Ama and Nani (Ama's mother) were in Quetta either to help the unfortunate woman to deliver a baby or to leave the world peacefully. Whatever their desire was, it brought the cyclones and storms in the life of my Ama. Right after ten days from her death, Nani came rushing to Ama, who was sitting in the kitchen and trying to feed Sobia with a milk feeder, and announced, "Cover your head Noor! Molana sahib is here."

Startled, Ama asked, "For what Ama jan?"

"For your *Nikkah!*" Nani replied hastily.

"Nikkah? With whom?" Ama shivered.

"Sultan *of course*!" Nani stressed on "of course", as Ama should have predicted that the death of her sister would going to bring curse on her.

"But he is my brother!" Ama protested.

"He *was* Noor!!! He *was*! Now he is going to be your husband. He is no more your *brother-in-law!*"

"Ama jan, what about my dream of becoming teacher? My education?" Ama cried.

"Noor!! Your nieces and nephews need you at this time! My grandchildren need a mother! How can you be so selfish?" Nani objected.

"But did you ask Aba? Why don't you write to him?" Ama knew that her Aba would never approve this marriage.

"Write? Are you in your senses? By the time the letter will reach him, *my* grandchildren will die mourning over their mother. I know your Aba, he won't object."

Ama stared at her for long time and before she could open her mouth, Sobia ran into the kitchen and announced, "Molana Sahab is here."

Ama covered her head with the small scarf she had around the neck, as her father never forced her to cover her head like other traditional men of her society.

Molana sahib came with documents; he stood at the door of the kitchen while the rest of the ladies hid their faces with their *dupattas.* Mulana asked Ama,

"Do you accept Muhammad Sultan as your husband with *haq mahr* of TWENTY RUPPEES??"

No one heard Ama saying yes, but they witnessed Ama signing on three pages with shivering hands. So eighteen years old Noor, *my Ama*, became mother of seventeen years old Sobia and the rest of them.

Five

All these events were narrated to me by Seema Khala. She came from Multan, one of the hottest cities of Pakistan, to Quetta, in search of work. She found the job in Aba's house just before three years before his first wife's death. She would visit Multan during winters but only for two weeks. She got married when Ama gave birth to Furqan. She brought her husband to Quetta too. They lived in the quarters at the back of our house. She didn't bear any children for thirteen years. As soon as I was born, right after thirteen years from Furqan's birth, Seema Khala got pregnant. She was certain that I *really* was a lucky fairy. She would always praise Ama for calling me Pari. Although, heart in heart, she knew that, apart from Ama, there was no one to name me. Aba was least interested in me, not because I was a girl, but because I belonged to Ama. Aba never accepted me and Furqan as his children and we both learnt that Aba had five children and we should have never tried to enter in that magical world. Seema Khala gave birth to Sitara, which means a star. She really was a star. Seema Kala sent her to Multan and her grandmother took care of her for years. It was a hard decision for Seema Khala, but she knew that if she kept her in Quetta then she would end up losing her job. To secure Sitara's future Seema Kala worked hard. Ama would always send her back to her home after lunch and Seema Khala would come back next morning at eight o'clock. During the hours that Seema Khala spent in quarter she would embroider bed covers, dresses and dining table covers in traditional Multani style. When Sobia got married Ama paid a good amount to Seema Khala for those handicrafts. This encouraged Seema Khala to sell her creations in the market. Slowly Seema Khala started getting orders from neighbors and merchants.

Ama and Seema Khala always avoided each other in presence of Aba. If they were sitting together and heard the sound of the door then one of them would make sure to hide in the kitchen or in a room. Main motive was only to show Aba that Ama was alone and wasn't sharing her traumas with anyone. Slowly I also learned to hide from Aba. Though he never spoke to me, sometimes he would take me in his car to move around the city: while I stared at passing cars I would wish to run to a place where there would be no Aba, no half siblings, no sharing: just me and Ama. My imagination became wilder with each passing day. Sometimes I would imagine myself dying and everyone rushing to see me, showering the love which they had always been hiding. Other time I imagined a charming man entering in our house and claiming me as his daughter, and I would pack my things and move to his house. I desired a house which would be my *home.*

I wasn't close to anyone in family. I loved Ama and she tried her best to pamper me, but there was no friend. In the days when Salma visited us with her children I used to be excited to have playmates, but slowly when Aba started showering love on them I prayed day and night they would go home. During the stays of Salma a game would start: "who showers most love?" One day Elias asked Asif, Salma's son, to ask all children to get ready. Ama dressed me in best pink frock which I wore once on Eid, I came rushing to Elias and said, "I'm ready!"

He looked at me from top to bottom and laughed hysterically and asked, "Where are your shabby jeans?"

"Ama said I should wear this," I replied.

"You are not going," he announced.

"But…"

"Come on, kids, let's go."

He never looked back. I went inside the room where Ama was folding the laundry. I lay down on bed and hid my face in the pillow.

"You will put wrinkles on your dress," Ama said.

"I am not going."

"Why?"

"I don't want to go with them," I replied

Ama never asked me the reason, as probably she knew it. She brushed my boyish haircut with her fingers, kissed my forehead and said, "Come on, change your dress, I'll make you fries and then we will read a story of *fairies*

The thought of fairies was enough to soothe my broken heart. Yes, a broken heart that I never showed to Ama, and she was the only person who didn't need to see it: she could read it.

The days I spent in school were miserable, too. I joined the Convent in kindergarten and completed my matriculation from the same school. In the Eighties it was considered as one of the best schools in the city, ran by organized missionaries; some of them were English who never went back to England. There was something making my life miserable, *racism;* not between different sects or religions, but between castes. I belonged to a rich Punjabi family, but the wealth of my father couldn't gain me respect. Punjabis were from the Punjab Province and they were settled in Baluchistan for different reasons: some were there for earning and other to escape from the hot weather of Punjab. Punjabis spoke Punjabi at home, but men were fluent in Baluchi and Pashtu, the two common regional languages. They adopted the Baluchi culture in their houses and for their dresses. The houses were decorated in traditional Baluchi style, with Irani carpets and rugs and cushions on the floor. The guest rooms were called *bhaitik,* and were separated for males and females. The living room was the separated part of the house used only to watch television, and in winters all three meals were served in the same room, on a long sheet spread on the floor. In summer, the afternoon lunch was eaten in the glass room. It was designed in such a way to absorb as much heat as possible during the daytime, as the summer period was shorter. There were two *glass rooms,* one where family members sunbathe while covered in clothes and the other for plants. Aba was fond of plants as much as he loved Quetta. He never accepted that Punjabis faced racism, he never did. He was a famous business man and was respected by all the tribal people. While he enjoyed the parties in tribal families, I suffered racism in school. During lunch break the Baluch children would rhyme, *"Punjabi gutter ki chabi!"*

"Punjabi is the key of gutter!"

That made no sense, but that was one of their favorite plays. I never understood who taught them such things. I never knew why they never sang some good rhymes from the Cambridge curriculum. They often yelled at me, "Punjabi, *dal khor,* lentil eater!"

They never accepted that Punjabis ate meat, too; they considered *dal* the food for lower class. I couldn't fight them, but I never told Ama about the mockery. She already had so much to worry for and it was she who taught me, through her silence, that it is best to wear a smile than to let melancholy dance on our face.

Six

Like every girl, Ama must have dreamed of a fairytale life, too. She would often call Furqan her Prince! Women are strange but most beautiful in the heart. They never stop expecting from men. When they are born they look upon their fathers to tell them they are princesses: if their fathers fail, then they wish to have love from their brothers. After sheer disappointment they dream of an ideal husband and finally they end up praying for a son. A man never loves a woman the way she desires, so either she accepts it and finds her own wings or she dies with the grief of being unloved throughout her life.

At night, when everyone would go to bed, Ama would stay up and talk to bhai for hours. Aba would often disapprove their closeness and call Furqan *aurat,* woman.

"Why are you clinging with her like a *saheli,* female friend?" Aba asked one day.

Furqan would open the mouth to answer back and Ama would interrupt him with an unexpected question.

"Will you eat *anday ka halwa, jee* egg dessert?"

I never heard Ama calling Aba with his name, the word *jee* would do all the work. Aba never called Ama with her name, Noor, and I was four when a teacher asked me my mother's name and I replied Ama. She asked me to go home and ask her name. That day I came to know that my Ama was Noor, The Light. But Aba had many ways of calling Ama. In normal days he would just yell, "*Sunti ho??* Are you listening??"

And Ama would get alerted as if the army had attacked. She would run on Aba's roar and in seconds she would be in front of him. Today, when I ponder and look back at it, I can't see them as husband and wife. Their relation was a perfect example of that between master and slave. There was no love, no understanding, and friendship was out of question. Aba preferred to sleep alone, but he couldn't have sex alone. Ama started to sleep in the lounge with Sobia and me on command of Aba. In a palace-like-house we were not given the freedom to have our own personal bedroom. Many years later I came to know that making a woman sleep in the center of the house is a proof of her virginity. In the middle of the night Aba would come in lounge and would take Ama with him. When Ama would come back I would stare at her from the corner of the blanket.

Did I ever get scared of marriage? I think no, I rather dreamt of a fairytale life and of a man who would love me perfectly. I never hated men; I rather thought their heart can be conquered at some point in life.

When I turned ten I started believing that I was mature enough to understand love. I became more and more expressive with all the people around me. One day I kissed Furqan's hand out of a sudden burst of love. He pushed me back and shouted, "Are you in your senses? Never touch my hand again! *Never!*"

"But I love you, Bhai!"

"Shut up!" and he left the room.

That day I learned that, as a girl, I shouldn't love a brother.

I planned to express my love for Aba. I asked Ama to teach me how to cook Aba's favorite dish.

"Pari, I'd be happier if you paid attention on your studies."

"Today only, *please*!" I said.

"Alright then, I'll teach you how to make *anday ka halwa*," she smiled and looked straight into my eyes. "But don't cry if Aba doesn't eat it."

"Does he hate me?" I asked.

Ama chose her words carefully, before giving me an appropriate reply. "No. He doesn't, Pari. It's just that he is choosy."

"*Acha,* OK, tell me, what do we need for *halwa?*"

And I gathered all the ingredients as Ama told me one by one. I set them on the kitchen table and Ama heated the oil in a pan; as she added cardamom I loudly said, "You didn't tell me we need *elaichi,* cardamom."

Ama smiled and replied, "It's your first time, Pari. Next time, *Insha'Allah,* by Allah's will, you'll be a perfect chef."

I think I blushed. I'm sure I blushed. The word *perfect* sounded so romantic to ten years old me. Slowly Ama kept on adding ingredients and I just stood there and handed her eggs, sugar and almonds. The *halwa* was entirely cooked by Ama, who was, without a doubt, perfect at cooking. In the evening, when Aba asked Ama to bring *chai,* tea, I rushed and asked her to give me *halwa* in the best dish. She asked me to choose any of my choice; I stood in front of the nine feet tall wooden cupboard with sliding glass door filled with crockery and cutlery from all over the world. It was all brought by Aba, as Ama never stepped out of the house. Aba was a perfectionist and each and everything in the house from plants to kitchen utensils were chosen by Aba. Things never got old in that house; they were replaced after every few years. Ama sometimes objected that such kind of expenditure was *israf,* waste of money, but Aba would shut her mouth with his most repeated dialogue, "Huh! Unthankful lady! When you married me you just brought a single suit, with you, in this house. You were just a beggar!"

And Ama would accept the fact quietly and patiently.

I stepped into Aba's room while reciting some verses from Quran, to save myself from Aba's wrath. Sometimes I thought the God doesn't live in the sky but in our very house. Mulana Sahib, who used to teach us Quran, only taught me Allah's *azab*. I learned that God is really strong, He loves throwing people in a pit of fire on every little deed, as Aba loves to throw things in the house on every little mistake of Ama.

"Aba, *halwa*," I found it hard to breathe and utter anything more.

He was reading a newspaper, one of his favorite activities to cut himself out from the world. He didn't listen, or probably pretended that he didn't hear. I tried to get the courage to repeat the words again. This time he looked at me from the back of his glasses and frowned at me.

"Leave here," he said.

I put the plate on the small round wooden table which was opposite to the maroon velvet covered sofas in the corner of the room and turned to leave the room.

Suddenly I found myself standing next to Aba and, staring at him, he noticed my presence and turned towards me and gave me an expression as saying, *"What the hell are you doing here?"*

I gulped and said, "I made this *halwa*."

"What for? Where was *that* lady?" he asked; by *that*, of course, he meant

Ama.

"I asked her to teach me how to…"

"Am I the object here to be used for experiments? Take this back."

I slowly picked the plate and left the room. I put the plate on kitchen table, quickly ran to the washroom and cried as long as I could. I washed my face and used the same technique of *cry and smile* of Ama's and came back to the lounge where Ama was sitting. She looked at my face and tried not to embarrass me by asking if I cried. She handed over me the plate with *halwa* on it and, while eating, she was continuously saying, "Masha Allah! What a good cook my Pari is!"

I smiled, because I knew I never cooked that *halwa*. I smiled, because I learned that day I *shouldn't* love any men of *that house*.

Seven

Ama had some magical personality: she never stepped out of the house, but women from neighborhood and relatives would come to see her. Their faces would be gloomy and sad when they entered in the house, and, after sharing each and everything with Ama, they would be laughing while sipping the tea. I never heard Ama's laughter, she would just smile lightly. She had the humungous patience of listening to ladies' affairs and giving advice on those matters. She would soothe them like she was their mother. I would look amazed at her and wonder how anyone could listen to so much of their stuff every day. She was always doing many things at once: cleaning, cooking, giving time to regular visitors, were few of her skills. She was skilled in gardening and had planted various plants in the garden. I never found any of her duties unfinished.

"How do you do so much work?" I asked one day.

"Allah helps me," she would say, as she would never give herself a credit.

"But why doesn't He help me in doing homework?" I complained.

"I love my work, Pari. You don't love your work."

"That's not true!" I protested.

"Really? So why are you always late for school?" She asked, and I turned speechless for some time.

"Because I miss you, there. I hate leaving you at home."

"But that's for few hours and then you come back home. Now, I have to fold the laundry. Come help me." She never wasted a single minute of her life. I never saw her hands resting, except when she slept, but even that for few hours.

"Ask Seema Khala to do that, I answered rudely.

"Very bad, Pari!! That's so rude. You know she works so hard and these are not her clothes."

"But she works here.." I started to say.

"Pari!" She was shocked and let the trouser fall and held me firmly from both my shoulders. It was the first time I felt anger in her voice.

"Never say anything like that again. She is your Khala, Aunt. She isn't a maid here but my sister."

"Real sister?" I got curious.

"Sort of. Let me put it like this, Allah says all humans are brother and sister to each other."

"Is Aba your brother?" I couldn't grasp the new information.

"Oh,Pari no. He is my husband."

"But you said he is your brother." I was confused.

"Oh forget it. Have you finished your homework, already?"

I didn't bother to answer. I hated any discussion which was related to school and studies.

"Ama!"

"Hmm."

"Why don't you also take admission in school?"

She probably thought I sounded innocent and held my face and kissed me. Getting a kiss was no less than an honor, as she was introvert in expressing love.

"I have completed ten grades in the school," she said proudly.

"We won't tell this to the principal and she will give you the admission." I was so proud of my idea.

"Why do you want me to go there? Kids will laugh at you."

"They already do," I replied sadly.

"Why?" She got suspicious.

"Nothing. Give me the dinner. I am hungry. I was her daughter and I wanted to be like her. Introvert.

"Finish the laundry with me and we will have dinner together." By together she meant all the family members except her. She would always eat at the end after serving everyone. I always missed eating with her and would always sit with her when she sat down for a meal. She never minded if the food was cold. She always seemed to enjoy her meal. I never knew what made her so happy after such a long hectic day.

I kept rolling the shirts like a ball, but she didn't mind. She would open them and fold them properly. She never shouted and would never get angry. She was full of magic and I would think, *I never need anyone. I have her. I have my Ama.*

Eight

I never knew how was the rest of Pakistan; even to think of it was a fancy idea. I imagined that Pakistan was some far distant land, a place which was magical and if I ever went there, then I would be lost in its hustle and bustle. I never believed that Quetta was part of this very country: it was hard to believe because the people shown on the only two channels broadcast on TV were different. They wore a perfect smile on their beautiful faces. A smile, which I never saw in my city, even less in my home. I would wait for six days to watch a children's game show at 4:00 PM every Saturday, not because I enjoyed it, but rather to see the children with their parents, to accept that not all the families are sad. To feel the love which existed in that far distant land. After the program Ama would often ask me what I watched. I never knew what to tell, as I only absorbed the idea of parents laughing with their kids, hugging them at the end of the show, carrying them in their lap. How does it feel to be held by your father? A touch, a touch I desired to have. How warm is that hug? I couldn't expect from Aba to give me love, but I would often tease Ama to let me kiss her. She was shy from everything; she probably lost her faith in gestures, in love, in cuddles. Every time I tried to reach her, I saw her face blushing.

"Pari, you will kill me."

"I just hugged you!!" I would protest.

"Your hug can crush the mountains." I would laugh and hug her again.

She was my Kabah, my worship house. I would swirl around her day and night. I never had courage to lose the sight of her. It killed me even if she would go to washroom. She was well aware of this, that she had pampered me, and she would often tell me, "Pari, now you should grow up, *bacha*, child."

"Why?" I would ask, while hiding my face in her lap.

"How will you live if I die?" She would ask in return.

I wouldn't fight on this question, because I believed that Ama couldn't die, she loved me like a God and Mulana said God doesn't die. Instead I would say, "If you die, I will sleep with you in your *qabar,* grave. "

And I always felt she smiled at my answer while ten-year old Pari hid in her lap. with this answer she would cover me with her *dupaata,* shawl.

"She will never leave me, Pari," I told to my other self. My imaginary friend, whose name was Parsatu, used to appear in my imagination under the shower and during afternoon plays. Children are always imaginative, but when they grow up in constant melancholy they end up becoming creators of masterpieces.

Nine

My childhood never had so much melancholy until a year later, on a day when Ama came home from the hospital after a check-up. She couldn't walk fast; she slowly lay down on the bed. Ama came home with Elias, who later told all of us that the doctor had told Ama her heart had become weak. Out of four, three walls had stopped working and she didn't have much time left. I saw Sobia, and Elias's wife, Asma, crying. I didn't understand much of what they said. I slowly climbed into the bed where Ama was lying and listening to all this. I wrapped my arms around her.

"So is she dying? She is really dying and I never knew it." I thought. I never knew why this news of her death was broken on her. For the first time I noticed she had lost so much weight. While lying around her I felt that I had hugged the bones only. She stopped talking and smiling. She distanced herself from me and I kept trying to get closer to her. I hated going to school, but once I came back I told her all the stories which could make her smile. But I failed.

"Pari go and play with Elias's son," she said one day.

"I hate him."

"*Naa..*No, Pari, Allah will be *naraaz,* disappointed."

"Why Allah sent him in our house? Everyone loves him. Even Aba."

Ama stared at me for long time until I had to avoid those looks. She was a mother who was dying and who knew that jealousy was growing inside me. She never told me that being jealous is bad. She always told me to be happy when others achieve something, rather than being jealous. But she never reprimanded me for being envious when I had to share love. I accepted this sort of jealousy as a good thing. I never had much to share. I had toys, but I never had to share them; unlike other children, toys never interested me much. But that year Allah was in a mood to try my patience. To try Pari, who was possessive about Ama.

On July 15th, Ama organized my birthday party. It was a small gathering and only my classmates and friends were invited. Ama couldn't participate, but she asked Sobia to buy me a fountain pen and a diary. Sobia wrapped the present and wrote on behalf of Ama,

"To Pari,

From your loving Ama."

Sobia insisted that Ama come inside, when I had to cut cake. Ama came inside for a fraction of a second, stared at me from the door and left. Later I came to know she was continuously vomiting. My friends seemed more worried than me. They insisted that I go and see her. I was selfish. I was too selfish. I wanted to play with them. I turned eleven that day and I felt it was *my day;* I was more interested in presents. I forgot my Qibla. I never saw Ama till everyone left in evening. With the approaching of silence my memory was retrieved. I went to Ama and showed her the presents.

"Did you like the pen and diary?" Ama asked.

"Yes, very much," I said truly. I meant it. I was happy to know that Ama knew I love pens and diaries; a diary which was to witness one of the most life-changing events of my life.

A month later, one afternoon, I was sitting near the pomegranate tree in our yard. I was keenly observing the ants playing (or running. My younger-self always thought ants loved to play). It was one of my favorite things to do. Since I came to know that Prophet *Suleiman*, Solomon, could speak to ants, I had a great curiosity to make these creatures talk to me. I envied him, for being so blessed to talk to animals, birds and insects, while I had no human to talk to. People often define childhood a care-free period but it's the one when the chances of feeling alone are high. Since the day Ama fell ill, I started feeling more and more alone, but there was something I wasn't ready yet. Ama's weak, fragile body, that was at least a kind listener which would hear my silly stories without a frown, was about to go.

On August 20th, Ama's condition started becoming worse day by day. Aba took her to the city's best hospital, but what I heard was that there was no heart transplant during nineties in Pakistan. *All over Pakistan.* That morning Aba took Ama to the hospital, and the doctors immediately admitted her. For eleven years old me it was still not possible to accept that Ama would not come back. And eleven years old Pari had to grow into twenty years old in one single day. That was destined; a destiny which isn't written but carved. In the evening, by mistake, I dropped some ink on bhai's papers. He would never talk much, because he was made that way, but if someone would touch his worthless possessions he would lose his cool. He scolded me as long as he had words and Ama wasn't there to tell me, "Pari, come sit with me and read to me." I suddenly felt I needed Ama around. I needed to hug her and kiss her till she would beg, "Pari, *bas,* enough." I started crying and had no control over my sobs. Aba always had resistance towards tears, and later, in the coming years, I learned all men have. He asked me to get ready to visit Ama. As a father, for the first time he understood the feelings of his daughter whom he never noticed. Aba, Sobia and

I reached to hospital. Ama was in ICU (Intensive Care Unit) and the doctors asked us to visit Ama one at a time and only for a minute. I was the last one to go inside. Before I entered, a nurse asked me to take off my shoes and wear the slippers. It was an O-shaped ICU and in the center there was a glass room where doctors were dressed in traditional army uniform. It was a Pakistan Army's hospital and was equipped with the latest equipment and doctors graduated from UK and USA. As I entered, I turned left as Sobia told me to do so, and on the first bed from the center I saw Ama. She had an oxygen mask on her face and needles in her hand. "How shall I kiss her?" I asked my imaginary friend. I don't exactly remember how long we kept staring at each other. Ama's eyes were empty; there was no pain and no love. She had nothing to say. I guess she was all ready for her journey, for the final one. She least cared to be visited by her most beloved daughter, her *prince*, all she wanted was to sleep. "Ok. I will go now." I said after a few minutes.

I saw she slowly moved her mask with her left hand and whispered, "Never worry anyone, Pari. Especially your father."

I nodded and said, "We will talk when you are back."

She smiled. Yes, I saw her smiling in that intense pain.

"Go, now," she said.

I turned to go and I stopped to kiss her. I saw in the central glass room a graceful doctor in *saree* staring at me. I found it a bit embarrassing, to kiss Ama in front of her. Secondly, I never wanted to possibly hurt Ama with my kiss, while she was attached to the machines. I looked at Ama and I couldn't smile. She kept looking at me. I reached to the door and gave her one last glance and there she was, still looking at me. As her eyes were saying, *Pari, the real journey starts now.*

At ten o'clock, when Sobia, Aba and bhai were watching the news in such aloud volume that talking to each other was impossible, the phone rang. The phone rang and my heart skipped a beat. The eleven years old Pari's sixth sense proved to be stronger than ever. I ran and picked up the receiver, "Hello."

"I am calling from AMH (Army Medical Hospital), can I speak to Mr. Sultan?"

"Why?" I heard myself asking such an unexpected question.

"Who are you?"

"I am *Mrs. Sultan's* daughter," I stressed on *Mrs.*

"*Beta*, child, call your dad."

I went to Aba and shouted in his ears as there was no other option.

"Aba, there's a call for you."

"Who is there?"

"I think a doctor, from hospital."

Aba quickly walked to the table in the corner where the phone was and answered it.

"Hello?"

I left the TV lounge and locked myself in Furqan's room which was next to the lounge. I tried not to listen. My heart was beating fast. I knew something was wrong. I suddenly heard Aba screaming, "Allah!",

I shut my eyes tight and wrapped my knees with my arms and hid my head in between them. The second sound I heard was that of the car's engine. Aba and bhai left while the house started echoing with a mourning sound.

An hour later Aba arrived with an ambulance, I went out and saw them bringing Ama wrapped in a white cloth and they laid her in the yard. She never walked anymore into the house where once she walked. She never called anymore my name. She entered like a stranger. She came back home on a stretcher, not on her feet. And that day I kissed her hands, face and feet as much as I could. She never said *Bas*. Then Aba came and I saw him crying, which surprised me. I never knew he would care. I went to him and he hugged me. I was startled, but I hugged him tightly. He said, "Now I'm your Aba and Ama as well." I couldn't believe Aba said that. But an evil feeling crawled in my heart and I suddenly felt happy that Ama died. I felt Ama's death could bring me all the love I always desired. While everyone mourned, I smiled till the dawn of the next day, until men took Ama for *namaz-e-janaza,* funeral.

Ten

Losing a mother is as if the trees lose their leaves in spring, it's as if a traveler lose his way and moreover it's to get lost in the sea and land on an unknown deserted island. Her absence opened the bitter doors of reality to me. It's strange how, in times of sorrows, the most familiar faces become unfamiliar. A funeral and the funeral processions are the only circumstances when one finds oneself in a crowd, while the rest of the time is made of desolated days. The rest are the days where we have to fight our battle alone, and the rest are the nights when we soak our pillow without a sound, without a cry. Mothers are strange beings: they shadow us day and night without complaining. Ama was the one who had been ill since I was born, but also had had the strongest will power. She'd never let me know what she was going through. Her smile never faded, her love never vanished until the last day. Her death wasn't bestowed on her: it turned home into a graveyard. Aba, who for the first time ever had showered love on Ama's coffin, made that love to be his last one. I knew men tend to forget their promises, but they can be as quickly forgotten as Aba's: that was the first time I realized it. Ama was that roof who protected me from al the storms and the typhoons. She never let me see behind the masked faces which became unmasked right after Ama's death. She faced all the harsh realities alone and portrait the world for me as a heaven on earth. As long as I was with her, I loved life. I imagined the world beyond the wall of my house as a paradise, this lead to me to an illusionary world which I believed existed outside the boundary of my house. I thought Ama's death would bring all the love which I missed all those years. Stories of parental love and love of relatives would bestow on me. My immature soul thought that Ama was the only barrier between me and the love that was in that outside world. As long as she was alive

I selfishly sought for more love. I never wanted to share her and I never wanted *only* her love. I wanted more. And more came on my way but just as a firefly which flickers and burns.

The first thing which started right after Ama's death was the visit of relatives from different towns and cities of Pakistan. People I never met while Ama was alive came to show their condolence. I was gladdened that I'd be loved so much. Death is celebrated as much as wedding, the only difference was the lack of music and dance. The expenditure on both costs equally. For next ten days the food was being ordered and three meals were served each day, not only in home, but sent to mosque and orphanage as well. Human attitude is one of the most astonishing features and I learnt it at that age. The close relatives would complain to a girl who lost her mother about not getting enough steak with curry. Some ladies often asked Salma to meet me, and Salma would find me playing in dirt with shabby hair and messy jeans. She would finger brush my hair and tell me to be decent and quiet. I hated that moment because I knew these ladies weren't interested in me, they only wanted to see how a eleven years old was doing without a mother. They showed sympathy but no love. They showed curiosity but no care. They would mercilessly ask me questions about whether I missed Ama. On the third day since Ama's death, Khala Samrina from the neighborhood visited us. Often, when I'd go to get my ball while playing cricket, she never opened the door. I was asked to see her as she had expressed her wish to meet the youngest, so I went in my shirt long till knees and loose pants. She jumped in place and exclaimed, "Ch ch.. where is your *duppata,* scarf?"

I didn't know what to answer her, as Ama never asked me to wear dupatta. All her life she would hide herself in black *burqa* (gown), but never once asked me to hide myself. She raised me like a boy and that day the crowd was gathered to change me. From my neighbors to my half siblings, their only concern was to scare me from Allah. To prove that I was strayed and Allah's wrath would fall upon me. Lastly, a day came when I lost all my faith in the love of relatives. Instead of being with me and Sobia, our visitors engaged themselves in shopping and dining out. They wanted to buy each and every dry fruit and Irani product available in Quetta. I would quietly see them coming back from shopping and packing the things. Finally, when they had enough of mourning, they started leaving us in those four walls, alone for the coming years.

My dearest *Khala*, Ama's sister, handed over me five hundred bucks before leaving. She never asked what I needed, whether I really needed the money or rather her. No one asked me what I needed. When I would make an excuse to cry on small matters they showered money on me. I never needed money. But they misjudged me. Sobia, who was furious at Khala for her indifference towards us, taunted, "So she trapped you with money, you *greedy*!"

This title was enough to haunt any person of my age. I shouted, "I'm not greedy!"

I threw the money, which I later discovered in Sobia's purse.

Eleven

The rest of the summer passed quietly and, like the tortoise, we all enclosed ourselves in our shells. Our communication confined only to meal and necessary tasks. As the autumn approached I found myself lonelier than ever. I started realizing how Ama's presence had been the source of mellifluous sounds, though she was a taciturn by nature, but her presence had been the cause of our loquaciousness. Life changes us in many ways, but the most painful result, on the life of anyone, is that to get matured at an early age. I quickly learnt that Aba hated tears, so the first time I cried after an argument with Sobia he came into the room and yelled, "Is this a home or a zoo?"

He would always roar like a lion, which was enough to stop anyone's heart. I lay down in a posture of fetus and tried not to cry. I couldn't control the sound of sobbing and running nose and the only solution Aba found to soothe his youngest daughter was to throw bills of rupees on me.

"Keep it and stop crying."

That day I learnt another lesson: crying in front of others brings no good. Tears had no power, they were as useless as my being. They were as useless as I was. There was no Ama to cuddle me and soothe me. That day I promised to myself to love everyone who would need me. I made a promise to God that if I would ever see any person crying I would never throw money on them. I would love them and prove them that love is more powerful than money. Life smiled on my childish oath and planned to prove me wrong.

The more I wished to stay away from home, the harder things got at school. Sarah, who was smarter and wiser than me, was my only friend.

Things in which I had no knowledge, there she provided me with wisdom. But her dad got transferred to Abottabad and she moved there. Before leaving she taught me how to operate computers. Soon we got our first home computer. For many days the only entertainment it provided us was the Media Player and Paint. Those two programs were no less than a luxury. Sobia would fight with me to watch Bollywood movies when Aba wouldn't be at home and that was the only time when I could use the computer. For Aba computer was no less than a porn movie itself. He thought that the use of computer was confined for a single purpose and any person using this machine had no character in his eyes. But it was Furqan who was a rebel and would quietly do what Aba would never approve. He would save his salary and spend all on his only sister. It was his idea to have our own personal computer and use it to excel in the field of education. He encouraged me to learn typing and other programs as they would help me in future.

One day, when Aba wasn't at home, Furqan brought his friend to connect the computer with the telephone line. So we had our first Internet which could only be used with 20 or more bucks of card. Slowly, with the help of Sarah, I learned to make my first Hotmail account and downloaded MSN Messenger. It opened a new world to me. In the middle of the night, when everyone would move into their room, I'd leave my warm bed and climb into an office chair and switch on the system. I started getting requests on MSN from new unknown friends. I would reject them, as I had a fear of being caught by Aba or Sobia. They wouldn't have killed me, but surely I would have been pulled out of the school.

One day, I fought terribly with Sobia who made a French toast and forced me to eat. I hated that toast and always believed that everyone in this world knows about it, but it was only Ama who knew that I would puke, rather than eating French toast. For Sobia it was quite an abnormal thing to not try that toast which she had made with so much effort. I was never used to be courteous; it was my first encounter to the fact that people can get hurt on little matters. That day Sobia and I lost all the respect and we fought like those wrestlers that Aba would see on TV. These fights continued till the day Sobia got married. Sobia wasn't much happy on her wedding, but she had no choice.

Sobia passed her high school and had an aim to enrol in the university. During that time there was only one university in Quetta which had co-education and Aba would always say that he would delightfully kill his daughters, rather than sending them in a place where men and women study together. I would often wonder whether there really were any girls in that university. I didn't know any family in my neighbourhood who sent their daughters to that university. Seldom would I read about few ladies in local newspaper who were working with NGOs and would be interviewed or featured in paper. I would stare at their photos for long time and imagine what kind of fathers they had. Didn't they consider sending their girls out of homes *haram*, forbidden? These questions only baffled me and there were no answers except a bitter compromise which every girl like Sobia had to make.

It was right after Ama's death that Sobia started receiving proposals. Proposals and arranged marriages are more like a fancy dress show, in which, after serving a good amount of food, a girl would be asked to come in front of a few ladies who would be close acquaintances of a boy looking for a wife. On such occasions, these ladies often forget that they are female too and should be careful in such sensitive matters. They would directly comment on Sobia's short height and tan complexion, but then Seema Khala would suddenly interrupt and say, "She has long beautiful hair, *MashaAllah*, till her knees!"

And then these ladies would demand to remove the duppata from Sobia's head, so that they could see her hair. Then they would comment on it.

Once, a lady with brown skin said, "She has beautiful hair but our *beta*, son, likes girls with fair complexion."

Each and every thing proved to me that I was dumb and I never had an ability to understand such things, like why boys need white skin and long hair in all the girls. Is marriage incomplete, without these physical traits? Why the proposals are more like buying fruits and veggies from the market? Unfortunately, all these questions had no answers and they are still a mystery in many homes. Sobia was never once asked what she wanted and what her wish was: she was considered as an ageing woman, whose marriage was an utmost issue.

One afternoon, I got a terrible pain in my stomach and legs: initially I thought I should keep it to myself, but then Sobia saw me cuddling myself. Rather than showing any sympathy she smiled and was a bit furious.

'Now I have to be your mom as well.'

"Who asked you to be my mom?!" I shouted

"Fine, then keep lying down until you fill your clothes with blood."

"Blood? What do you mean?!" I wanted to cry.

And there she explained me that I had entered into a new phase of my life which is apparently a sign of maturity but more like being a baby. Soon, on the same day, I got my first menstrual cycle which took away all my confidence. I felt so vulnerable and embarrassed, that it is such a filthy thing to face. Sobia said she would give me some cloth and cotton to use for sanitation. Suddenly she discovered that there was no cotton and she had to get it from pharmacy. Sobia asked Seema Khala to bring a cotton roll, but Seema Khala asked her to accompany her, as if any man who had seen a lady going alone would consider her of less moral values. Sobia was too scared to leave the house, as fearing that if Aba would know, he with no doubt would bury her under our pomegranate tree. I never wanted her tomb in our house, as graves had started haunting me since I saw Ama's. It wasn't the first time Sobia was going out with Seema Khala without Aba's notice, for her it was an adventure, she considered herself as Hercules, every time she would come back and remove her *burqa*. When she was sure that she wasn't caught by Aba, then she would laugh hysterically and say, "A house from where not a bird can fly out without Aba's permission. Only Sobia can go out."

"One day he will find you and kill you with his gun," I would say.

"You will be the one to cry the most. As it's me, who protects you from him."

"First protect yourself!"

And she really couldn't protect herself. She went to the pharmacy, where she met for the first time Mohsin, who was working there. When Sobia entered with Seema Khala and saw him, her heart missed a beat. She was too scared to look at him again. She had lot of fears and, out of many, was that he could spread the news in the neighbourhood that Sobia was staring at him. She was always taught one important lesson: character is all that a girl has.

Mohsin wrote his name and the phone number on the receipt and put it in the plastic bag. He looked at Sobia and smiled. She came back home and explained to me all the procedure quickly. I continued crying, "How will I walk in school?"

"God! You haven't lost your legs!" she got tired.

Seema Khala came in the room and started laughing.

"Why are you laughing? You all hate me!" I cried more.

"Now if you will continue crying your Aba will come and would know what has happened. If he knows you are a woman, now, he will find a husband for you." She exploded another bomb and Sobia started laughing and singing wedding song.

"Ama!" I cried, and started calling Ama.

"Sobia you go out of the room. Stop teasing her."

Seema Khala explained me everything and soothed and encouraged me by telling me about how strong I was.

Days passed by and I started noticing that Sobia would always be on the phone, when Aba would go out. Seema Khala didn't notice, as Sobia would always say that she was talking to her friend Mariam. I started becoming suspicious, as at first the phone would always ring for once, and a second time for longer. I started spying, not because I was interested to know, but in a fear that, if it was really a guy, then Aba would kill both of us together. But as the days passed, Sobia stopped showing any interest in talking to me or Seema Khala. I started becoming lonelier than before. At least, before, we would fight, but then I stopped seeing her. Aba would come home in the afternoon for lunch and after a nap he would go out for a walk. He would sit with us only in the evenings, but in his presence no one would say a word. There were only two channels on Television; it was before cables took over. There were dish antennas, but it was immoral, in the eyes of Aba, to have one in home. He would only watch news at 9:00 PM and we would either sit quietly or find some work to show that we were busy. Aba would have dinner right when the weather forecasts were broadcast and exactly at 10:00 PM he would go to bed: I never knew at what time he did sleep, because his consciousness was always awake. One slight moment and he would be up.

Sobia Started getting calls day and night. There were two telephone sets: one upstairs, in Aba's room, and one downstairs, in TV lounge, and the word "mobile phone" was not known by any of us. One day, during the morning, when Aba wasn't at home, Sobia got the call. I went upstairs and quietly held the receiver and heard a masculine voice on other side. I was shocked and scared and I heard Sobia's voice, "Mariam, I'll call you afterwards." She put down the phone and the other person didn't say a word. He got the signal Sobia gave in code. I thought maybe Elias or Seema Khala would have intruded in Sobia's secret business. Before I could go out, Sobia entered the room and slapped me on my face. I got shocked and started to cry. She screamed and shook me, "Stay quiet! I don't want any noise. Why did you pick the phone?"

"Who were you talking to?" I yelled.

"None of your business!" She gave me another slap, "Next time, don't ever try to do that!"

I would often be tortured by her, but that day I lost my cool. "First you stop that!" I screamed.

"Lower your voice!" She raised her hands to hit me once more, but that day I held her hand and shouted,

"ENOUGH!!! If you ever touch me again, then I will tell Aba everything!"

She stared at me in shock, and, after a little while, she started crying, which was not unusual. I sat down giving up and asked politely, "Who is he?"

"Go to hell! May you never get peace! Go and die!"

I looked at her and shrugged, "Same to you."

It was enough hatred for that day. I kept myself busy in school homework or reading. I sometimes would sit with Seema Khala and ask her to tell me the stories from her childhood. She would repeat the same old stories told hundred times and it was always a better option than to sit and die of boredom. Sometimes, when Seema Khala would be busy, I would walk from one room to another and think of Ama. I would touch her things to feel her presence and would think why Allah never took me with her. I used to think I will die with Ama and sleep in her hug in the grave. It was so strange that I was living and breathing without her. God left no choice and never replaced Ama.

One day Sobia left home with Seema Khala for shopping clothes for summer. Aba told them to get back in an hour. Once they returned,

Sobia quickly rushed to her room and left the shopping bags there and came out. Few days later, I saw a new perfume in her cupboard and a dry rose. I asked her once again, "Who is he, Sobia? I am worried for you."

And I really was. Sobia asked me to swear that I wouldn't tell anyone, and I promised. She started telling me about Mohsin who worked in the chemist shop.

"What's his cast?" I asked, because I knew Aba would never marry her in another cast.

"Baloch."

"What??" My jaw dropped. "How will Aba ever agree to his proposal?"

"Neither his family." She was saddened.

"Then, what will you both do?"

"I will never marry," she got emotional.

"If Aba listens to you, he will find a man and marry you."

"Shut up!"

To win her heart I told her that I would pray for her, but I never did.

Twelve

One day, Sobia looked worried, so I asked her what was wrong.

"Mohsin is in a political party. Baloch Association."

It was an association working for Baloch Liberation. They wanted all Punjabis to leave the state and wanted Balochistan as a separate country.

"Great. Another breaking news."

"Go to hell!"

"Ask him to leave it, if he loves you."

"He says he would, but I don't think so. He is so much involved in the party!"

"Sobia! You have to force him. He is wasting his time."

"He is very caring. He doesn't sound political. He joined the party because his uncle forced him."

"But he has to find a way to get out of it. Ask him, when you speak next time."

She started pondering.

One morning I was still sleeping when I heard Sobia screaming. She was hysterically crying and everyone got up. Seema Khala ran and took her in her arms,

"What happened?"

"He died!" She screamed.

I froze and looked around and thankfully Aba and Taimoor hadn't come in the room. Seema Khala understood that something was wrong and put her hand on her mouth,

"Quiet! For God's sake, be quiet! Your Aba will kill all of us!" She turned to me, "You, take care of her, and I will tell your Aba that you both fought!" I knew Aba would scream at me but I didn't mind. I hugged Sobia, "Calm down. Shh.. What happened?" I whispered.

"He died!" She was in tears.

I cried too and asked, "Who told you? How?"

"His friend called and I answered quickly, as last night he didn't call. His friend told that he was shot by a member of his own party. They argued on something and the other shot him in rage." She burst in tears.

In the meanwhile, Seema Khala was asking Aba about breakfast: she had controlled the situation and this relaxed me.

"What if he was lying?" I asked Sobia.

She looked at me thoughtfully.

"I'll ask Seema Khala to go to the chemist's shop. If there is something, she would know", I said.

"But, she..."

"She knows, now, after what just happened. Please, now, don't cry."

I went inside the kitchen and told Seema Khala everything. She looked at me baffled and angrily.

"Why you never told me this before?"

"You know, Seema Khala. Sobia never let me, else you know her."

I looked at her and tried to read her thoughts, "Khala please go to pharmacy."

She looked at me and said, "Let your Aba go to work," she whispered.

After Aba left, Seema Khala wore the black gown and hid herself from head to toe and asked me to go with her. I went inside and told Sobia to wait. She was continuously crying. We went to the pharmacy and it was closed. We asked a person standing out why it was closed, "The owner's son has died last night."

"The one who used to work here? "Khala asked.

"Yeah, the same guy. He was killed last night."

"What was his name?"

"Mohsin. He was such a nice boy," he said with pity.

We started walking back home. I turned to Khala and asked, "Now what will we say to Sobia? She will cry again!"

"Say that nothing has happened. We saw the boy in pharmacy and he ignored us. Tell her he betrayed her."

"She will still mourn!"

"But she will forget, eventually. One can hate and forget a person who betrays, but one who dies can never be hated." I didn't understand, but I stayed quiet.

When we reached home Sobia had locked the room, and we heard no sound. I looked at Khala and she said, "Go, lock the main door." I ran and locked the door, as everyone had left and we were alone at home.

"Sobia, open the door!" Seema Khala shouted and she turned to me, "Pari, get me a hammer."

I ran into the kitchen and started searching the drawer where all the tools were kept. I found one and gave it to her. She started hitting the nut door latch. It was an old lock so it didn't take much effort to break. When Khala entered inside she screamed, "Sobia!"

I ran inside and I saw Sobia lying on the floor, and on the floor there were medicine strips. She was still conscious and crying badly. Seema Khala took her to the washroom, and made her vomit; she was prudent, and avoided to call anyone. Khala knew that calling someone would not do any better but only worsen the situation. If Aba had gotten the slightest inkling that Sobia had an affair, he would have killed all of us. I fetched the water bottle on Khala's instruction, and she forced Sobia to drink and vomit. I stood there and watched Khala's struggle with Sobia and I believed that Khala certainly was some professional doctor. Once she got sure that Sobia's stomach was clean, she took her to the bedroom. Sobia was able to walk, though crankily. Once she laid her down, Khala softly said to Sobia, "My child, he is okay. Why didn't you wait for us to come back?"

She started sobbing again and, in tears, she pointed to the morning newspaper lying on the floor, "You are lying! I read the news! I saw it with my own eyes. They killed him! They killed my Mohsin!"

I looked at her strangely and I thought how she could call someone her own, when she never had any relationship. I decided to stay quiet. Khala forced Sobia to sleep for some time and she definitely was sleepy. No pain and tragedy can make us stay awake for many days. Sleep overcomes us in all the pain. Once she fell asleep, we quietly left the room and went to the kitchen. Khala looked drained and exhausted.

"Khala you go and rest, I'll cut the vegetables," I said.

She smiled and looked at me, "I'm okay Pari. I wish your mother was alive. Now Sobia should get married as soon as possible, and I will go back to my hometown."

I looked at her with surprise. I wanted to scream and ask *what about me?* But I stayed quite. I had never been good at asking for love.

"I will start finding some suitable proposal for her," she added further. "What if she does that again?"

"We have to keep an eye on her, from now on."

I stayed quiet.

"You should have told me, Pari," she stopped peeling the turnips, and turned to me.

I felt guiltier. *It's all my mistake.*

Sobia slowly got detached from everyone in the house. She would only communicate when she needed something. At one time the house would chant with her voice, but then we would not even see her often. She locked herself in the room and would not come out even if Aba was at home. Slowly he started noticing Sobia's absence and would often show the suspicion through his satirical words, "Where is Sobia?"

"In her room," I would answer.

"Is she?"

"*Jee?* What?"

"I haven't seen her for hours. Is she really at home?"

I would quietly leave the room and would go and beg Sobia, "For God's sake. Just go out of the room and show your face to Aba."

"I don't want to."

"He will kill you," I would warn her.

"Better."

"We all are suffering because of you. You chose that man, now you face all this!" I would lose my temper and regret it later.

"Who has asked you to suffer for me?"

She wasn't ready to accept it and I didn't want to argue. Facing Aba almost seemed a better choice than arguing with her, making her cry and then consoling her.

One day, Seema Khala came with news that some people were coming to see Sobia. Aba was neither indifferent nor eager; he gave the money to Khala and asked her to make the arrangement. In the evening, some ladies appeared as if they were in fancy dress show. They ate snacks, had tea, and then demanded to see the girl. They never cared passing a comment on her 5.3 height which was too short for their 5.9 brother;

they even asked why she had a pimple on her forehead. They left on a note that they would let us know. This became a regular routine and people started coming and going out, leaving us with the bitterness of their words. They were looking for Miss Universe for their ordinary looking brothers and sons. Sobia, who was already emotionally broken, started becoming bitter and doleful. The only option which was left was to send her to Sibi at Salma's place. Seema Khala called Salma and told her everything and begged her to do something before Aba could come to know anything. Elias and Furqan already started noticing a change in Sobia and she was not at all willing to change. Seema Khala took the permission from Aba to send Sobia to Sibi, she told that Salma was not well and children's exams were going on. Aba gave the permission, but he wasn't happy at all. For him it was a taboo, that a girl spends a single night out of home.

After a week since Sobia's departure, Salma informed us that the cousin of her husband was interested in marrying Sobia. It probably was because Salma was given lot of dowry and that was the attraction he found in Sobia. I was convinced that Sobia would never agree, but I was shocked when I got the news that she accepted the proposal. When she came back to Quetta, I asked her why she accepted the proposal. She answered "Do I have any other option?"

I definitely had no reply.

There was no communication between Sobia and her fiancé. Aba was not in favour of it and considered it as a vulgarity. A few days before the marriage, Seema Khala came in room and started advising her, "See Sobia, what's done, is done now. Don't ever tell anything about Mohsin to your husband."

She didn't comment.

"No matter how much your man says that he is your friend and you can trust him, never ever tell him about the past. Men can't bear such things."

"What if he tells her about any girl?" I couldn't control.

"You keep your mouth shut. Don't interrupt your elders," she scolded me.

\A day before the marriage Aba called Sobia and asked her to sit down,

"Sobia, tomorrow you will be in your new home. It's your duty to take care of those people and especially your husband. You must never leave that house. Only after your death you can leave that house."

With this message, Aba sent his daughter to that stranger's house.

The next day she got married. She never told us anything about her family or her husband: even if Salma Khala asked, she preferred to stay quiet. She said she was happy and we should not worry. *She has taken Aba's advice seriously,* I would think. *I'll tell you, Aba, you can't rule everyone. No, Aba, no. I will fly and never come back.* Rebelliousness started to grow in me.

Thirteen

It's hard to say that time flew by and I grew up, as nothing has been lost in the mist of time. I registered each and every moment and its marks on my soul. Each day was spent in fear, in loneliness, in prison.

Seema Khala left for ever. She said she had fulfilled her responsibilities, which were left behind by Aba. She left my responsibility in the hands of Asma's, who was already bearing Elias. There was no point in persuading Khala to stay, as her own daughter was growing fast and she needed to care about her future. Khala left and I was left in the same old world with a new experience of isolation. Asma got pregnant for the second time, after a month Khala left, and we decided to divide the responsibilities. Aba never seemed to be happy with our services, and I couldn't understand how to keep him happy.

I started working hard in school and my grades improved dramatically, but Aba never seemed interested. He would always criticize me for not getting 100 out of 100. I kept trying, but I could never discover how to get 100 in every subject. I stopped showing him my report cards. I kept talking to my imaginary friend, but I never told anyone. I was no more a child and that made me ashamed, too. I grew my imaginary friend and, this time, I imagined that was my messenger from Ama. Deep in my heart I knew it was a charade, but I kept it to escape from the bitter reality.

One day, my English teacher, Miss Zeenat, called me out of the class. I got worried and my hands started sweating. I wasn't concerned about having done something wrong. I liked her. I always had wanted to talk to her, but I never had the courage. When she called me, I felt like if I was going to talk to some boy. I never understood why my heart beat so fast, and why I was trembling. I followed her and we went to the corridor.

"Pari, your notebook." She handed me my English notebook.

"Yes, ma'am. Is something wrong?"

She took the notebook back and opened it from the right, on the last page which was filled with sketches. All were of a girl, the outline of her face and in some of them she was sitting on a beach. I smiled, when she showed me those. *She saw them!* My heart danced with joy. I intentionally drew those on the English notebook, after Faiza, my class mate, commented on them when she saw my rough notes. "They are really cool. You should probably talk to the art teacher, she might ask you to draw something for the notice board. You will be famous, Pari!" Faiza tempted me. I didn't know the art teacher, as I was not taking art, but I really wanted to impress Miss Zeenat. I wanted to talk to her, for once, but all my confidence would vanish, when I would see her. I think she knew it, because she would often smile at me, if I saw her in the corridors or staffroom.

"There's nothing wrong. They are beautiful drawings."

"Thank you," I smiled.

"Why don't you draw the face of these girls?" She asked.

I recalled Ama told me once that on the Day of Judgement Allah will ask us to put life in the objects we drew.

"It's prohibited in Islam," I replied hesitantly.

She smiled, "Alright. Don't draw faces, but for drawing use the sketchbook. This is your English notebook."

Though she was smiling, I couldn't understand whether she was annoyed or even only teasing me.

"I will."

"Good," she said, started to walk.

I wanted to talk to her once more, "Ma'am."

She turned, "Yes?"

"Is it okay if... I draw something and I share it with you?" I asked hesitantly.

She smiled and looked at me thoughtfully, which embarrassed me. "Sure," she said, and walked away.

I was on cloud nine and that happy mood followed me all day long. I wanted to buy a sketchbook, but I had no money. I went to Furqan that afternoon, "Furqan, I need some money."

"I have none."

I was saddened. I always had the problem of the tears flowing with every little hurt.

"Now don't cry!" He got upset. "Okay, tell me, what is it?"

"I need a sketchbook," I said.

"I'll get you tomorrow," he promised.

It was a long wait, but I had to bear with that. Next day, after coming back from school, I started waiting for Furqan to come back. When he came home, I ran to his room. He looked tired so I thought to ask something else before asking for sketchbook.

"Bhai, do you need some water?"

"Yeah, get me a glass."

I wanted him to say no, but he didn't show any formality. I ran and fetched the water. I handed over him the glass and he gulped it in one breath. "One more," he gave me the glass back.

I was furious, but I had no choice. I ran back and got another glass.

"Here," I handed over him the glass.

He drank and gave me the glass back without any thanks.

"Have you bought the sketchbook?" I asked quickly with nervousness. *I don't want to hear a no*! I told myself.

"I just came from the university. You know that."

I was broken-hearted, as if he had given me some tragic news.

"Please, bring it in the evening," I requested.

"I will, Pari!" He took off his shoes and socks. "March, now! I have to take a shower."

I left his room and I started counting the minutes to six o'clock. After lunch he would always take a nap and then he would get up, watch TV and finally leave at 6:00 PM to see Tipu. There was no chance he would specially leave earlier for my sketchbook. Around six, when he was leaving home, I ran to the door and shouted from the back, "Bhai! Don't forget to buy my sketchbook!"

"Oh Pari, I know. I know." He was definitely irritated, but I least cared.

"What would Miss Zeenat think, for I haven't shown her anything, this week? I need to draw something fast and fill the pages!" I said to myself. In the evening, when Furqan came back, I eagerly looked at his hands. He was carrying a plastic bag, which indicated he didn't forget. I grabbed it and started flipping the pages, I took out my pencil case and I started to draw. Since then I started polishing my skills in drawing and would often show my work to Miss Zeenat, until, one day, Asma complained to Elias that I wasn't helping her in chores. She told him in detail that I was always busy with sketching and other activities which she considered useless. Elias got furious and came to my room. Seeing me sketching made him angrier and he snatched it and went to the kitchen. He lit the flame of the stove and set my book on fire. Tears kept rolling down my cheeks and I couldn't protest. That night, I crouched down with my pillow and kept calling Ama while silently crying. *Why you ever had to die? Why God ever had to take you?* I never heard from her and I kept praying she would visit me in my dream, but she never did.

I started to get Miss Zeenat's attention through other means. I started working harder on my English lessons and would always participate in class discussions. Either it was the effect of teenage or lack of attention, I started sending her greeting cards. She noticed that I was trying to find excuses to talk to her and this slowly spread among her colleagues. She must have been embarrassed, so she decided to ignore me. One day I kept the card in the notebook I handed her and next day she returned the checked work, but she didn't return mine. In English period she came in class and, before starting the lesson, she called my name, "Pari Sultan, here is your notebook. I found a card inside it. Pay attention to your studies, rather than writing emotional cards." All the girls looked at me and started whispering. I couldn't look up and, pulling my tears back, I took the notebook and went to my seat. When the bell rang for the break, all the girls started deriding at me.

"Oh, God, you are so childish!" I heard a voice at my back. I dared not to look back. When I went to the canteen, a group of girls followed me there and kept whispering.

"Hey, Pari, how many cards did you send her?"

"You only found a teacher to waste money on, seriously?" Another said and the rest chuckled. I stood in the queue and bought a packet of crisps. I went back to class, rather than staying with others.

"You should have told me, Pari." The voice was familiar. I snuck a peek over my shoulder and I was relieved to find Faiza standing there. After Ama's death I had no closest friend and barely I would sit with someone otherwise would be alone, as, whenever I joined any group, they would kick me out next day. After Sarah, I couldn't make any close friend. I started having my lunch alone and would silently talk to my imaginary friend. I was glad to see Faiza, as she was only one with whom I spent a few breaks when her best friend Eliza got absent. They both never mingled with others, though Faiza was quite sociable. Eliza always showed her disapproval if Faiza ever tried to bring a new friend in their group of two, and so she never appreciated my friendship with Faiza. She was possessive and I never blamed her. We all become possessive, when we have someone valuable and rare. When we are loved and cared by someone who is loved by so many we start feeling insecure. We grow a fear of losing them, and in that fear we start dominating in the relation, we close our fist tight to hold the sand of love, but what we don't understand is that that sand has already slipped from our hand. The birds we love break the cage and fly, before we could know.

I turned around and looked at Faiza, "I never thought it was important," I said.

"Yeah it isn't, but you know these girls."

"I don't understand... why are they so concerned?"

She held my hand and we started walking. I offered her crisps, but she replied with a "no" by shaking her head.

"They all like Miss Zeenat, but they never had guts to talk to her."

"I shouldn't have given her that card."

"It's okay. Don't think about that. I gave a bunch of flowers to Miss Lee, months ago!" She laughed.

"The history teacher?" I was surprised.

"Yeah! See what a risk I took."

She really took the risk and I couldn't stop admiring her for that. Miss Lee was in her forties, but she always looked not a day over twenty-five. She was from China and was also the head of the department of the secondary section. I liked her, too, but I preferred to be prudent, in her case.

"Now I have to face Miss Zeenat and all these stares throughout the year."

"You don't have to think about that: they will eventually forget if you let them."

"Means?"

"It means that if they noticed you are running away from them, then they would keep teasing you and will always remember. If you pretend that nothing has happened, then they will forget."

"You are so wise. How?"

"I don't know. I like spending my time with grownups"

"Hmm."

I had nothing to comment. I went back to the class and when the girls tried to laugh at me I laughed back. They didn't reply back and I thanked Faiza in my heart. I went home and put my new sketchbook, which I bought after skipping my lunches at school, in the cupboard under the pile of old books. Miss Zeenat's anger was right but her action wasn't painstaking. Looking back at that incident taught me one thing: that she could have found some other way to reprimand me. I never dared to talk to her ever again. I pretended as if nothing ever happened and she pretended I never existed in the class. That year at school became intolerable for me. I tried to replace Ama through her, but she couldn't understand that. I learnt another lesson, mothers are irreplaceable.

Fourteen

After finishing the high school I announced at home that I was going to study in university. Furqan was certain that Aba would never let me step out and Asma, who was the mother of two, by then, thought I should be married. One of my teachers informed me that the federal government had announced the scholarship for provincial students. I went to the college and gave her the copies of my documents, and I requested her to mail them. She was a kind lady who was unaware of my family issues. She always considered me as a happy-go-lucky and would often tell me how blessed I was to have a family and a home.

"Pari, you should always cherish the blessing of having a home and a family. I understand that mothers are irreplaceable, but you have a father who surely loves you."

I always showed that I agreed with her.

After few days a mailman came and brought the letter for the scholarship interview. Aba was not at home and Asma was busy with kids. I hid the letter and at night I went to Furqan's room.

"Furqan, I need your help." I sounded sheepish.

"Now what have you done?"

"I got an interview."

"What? For a job?"

"No! A scholarship. To study in Islamabad."

He laughed, "Go and sleep!"

"I am serious!"

"Are you insane? Do you even know what you are talking about?"

"I know. Leaving this house."

"He will kill you."

"Let's see," I shrugged. "Please, take me there on Monday."

"No."

"I am not even sure if I get it or not. Just let me try."

He thought for a moment and then agreed. Probably, he thought there were least chances that I would get a scholarship, as there were many students far more brilliant than me.

Before sleeping I prayed after long time,

"Allah, please, get me this scholarship and I will never ask for anything."

God probably smiled. I did not know that we, humans, never stop asking and He never stops giving.

On Monday, early morning, I went to Aba's room and told that I wanted to go to my school to meet my junior class teacher as it was her birthday. Aba knew that teacher and her family well, so he didn't ask any questions. He called Furqan and asked him to take me there and wait outside the school. I went to the Woman's College and Furqan waited in the visitors' room where many parents were already sitting. I was called in a classroom where the panel, comprised of six people, was sitting. I had no idea if they were teachers or government officers. They asked me several questions regarding my plan to study in the future and my educational background. One of the interviewers, while looking at documents, asked, "Miss Pari Sultan, daughter of Sultan Malik, right?"

"Yes Sir," I replied.

"Well your financial background is strong and your father can afford your education without any burden, then why did he send you for scholarship?" The satire was clear in his voice.

I thought for a moment and then opened my mouth, "He didn't."

"Pardon?"

"He didn't send me here, Sir. He doesn't know I am here."

"So you are telling me you are here without his permission. How would you go to Islamabad, if he doesn't give you his consent?"

"Like I came here."

Member exchanged looks with each other and were unsettled.

"Sir, I know he would never allow me to go to the capital. He won't even pay for my studies and at the end I would get married like my two older sisters. If I got the scholarship, I could step out without worrying for financial issues as this scholarship would cover my education and hostel expenses. At least I could help in setting the example for other parents, and I'm sure one day my father would realise that I was right. But right now, he won't, " I spoke in a flow.

After few more questions, they asked me to go, "You will be notified through mail in a week or two if you get accepted."

I thanked them and left the room.

Since that day, I started waiting for the mailman. I would go and check the mails every day, but I would come back disappointed. By the end of the week I lost my hope and was almost accepting the rejection, when on Thursday morning I got the letter of acceptance. I danced around and broke the news to Asma. She looked at me and continued doing her work, "I am so glad for you. It's good you got the scholarship. Don't be sad, if Aba doesn't let you go, as being selected is more than enough."

I didn't reply and danced from one room to another and celebrated my victory alone. When Furqan came home I showed him the letter. He got surprised and happy.

"Wow, Pari! You are better than all of us!"

"What about Aba?" I was happy seeing his reaction, as I had expected the same response of Asma's from him.

"Well, I will tell him."

I was surprised and startled. I couldn't believe that he decided to stand by my side.

At night, he went to Aba and told him about my scholarship.

"Are you silly? Have you lost your mind?" He roared like a lion, and my heart jumped. I wanted to go inside, but I decided to wait.

"Please, Aba, let her study. She will come back and would marry, one day. But for now, please, let her do what she wishes," he begged.

"If she wants to go, she can! I don't care! I will not see her face ever more in my life!"

He will calm down, I thought. After a month, I left for Islamabad in railway train. That was the longest and first journey of my life. Furqan accompanied me, but Aba never saw my face, before I left home.

It was my first journey by train and Furqan told me it was more than 600km of distance from Quetta to Islamabad. Furqan had often travelled out of Baluchistan to visit grandma. He was guiding me like a professional guide and was proud of his knowledge.

"There are so many tunnels and it will get dark when the train will pass under each one of them."

I was definitely excited.

"When will they come?" I asked like, a three year child.

"Keep looking out. You will see!"

I stared out and I saw a giant wall with a circular opening approaching us. It was like a huge alligator with open mouth and it gulped the train. It all got dark, as we really were in the alligator's stomach. I took a deep breath when I saw the light approaching. Although there was air on the train, but I was suffocated. Nothing is better than to see light after prolonged darkness. It was mesmerizing at the same time and I started waiting for more. I wanted to test my courage, to examine if darkness scares me or not. That time, I desired for darkness, while heading towards light.

"There is one tunnel which is 3.5 or 5.9 km. It's the longest."

"Wow! When will it come?"

"It's near."

I started waiting and once we approached I looked out and I felt myself near the sky.

"Are we so high?"

"Yes, 1900 metres above the sea level."

I put my hand out of the window and let the air pass through my fingers. It was an amazing feeling which gave a sense of freedom. I was a free bird. I realized how beautiful the world is. The mountains, the sky, the breeze and so much more, to sooth our eyes with the beauty made by God. All my life I looked at those mountains from a distance and that day I was close to them. I was among them and those giant rocks seemed to welcome me in their vastness. Once the sun started setting down, I got tired and sleepy. I climbed up the berth and stretched my legs and slept. Furqan woke me up once the train had stopped at some station.

"Get up, the train will stop here for thirty minutes."

We stepped down on the station, where some hawkers were selling snacks and some were selling toys. It was almost two in the morning and the sky was pitch black, but it was so different from the nights I had seen in my life. The nights in my life were always quiet and dark. People never went out of their houses after 11:00 PM but on that station even at 2:00 AM there was the atmosphere of a festival. I freshened up in one of the public toilets and suddenly homesickness overcame me. The bad smell of the restroom made me think of fresh and clean aroma of my home. I craved for home and suddenly missed Aba. *Will he be missing me? I shouldn't have left him. I'm a despicable daughter.* My conscience started filling my heart with guilt, so, to push its voice back, I turned to Furqan, "I want to buy a magazine."

"I will get one. Which one do you want?" He seemed to be in a good mood.

*"Taleem-o-Tarbiat, "*I told him the name of children's magazine of Urdu language.

"Going to university and still reading children's magazines!" He laughed.

The only reason to read that magazine was to feel Ama with me. She had introduced me to that magazine before I started reading. She would read to me every day, until one day she said, "Pari, my eyes are getting weak. From now on you will read and I will listen to the stories." And she made me addicted to reading. I started smiling, recalling the golden memories.

"You go and sit in your coach and I will bring the magazine," Furqan ordered and I obeyed. He was against the idea of going to shops with a woman. If any man would stare at me, he would lose his temper. Over protectiveness was in his blood and culture. He grew up in Baluchistan and there were least chances he would change.

We reached to Islamabad after a travel of two days and we stayed at a relative's home. She was Shia Muslim, a cousin of Ama: every year she would go to Iran to visit the shrine of Imam Raza and other martyrs and would take the chance to visit us for a day or two. After Ama's death she never visited us anymore, like many of our relatives we stopped seeing. Furqan had called her a week before without telling anyone and she had told him that she would have been very happy to have us. We reached to Rawalpindi station at night and went to Aunt's home. Next morning, after the breakfast, we took a cab and went to the university. After the submission of the documents they allotted me a room in the hostel.

Fifteen

Life started running faster than I had ever imagined. I would call home once in a week, but Aba never spoke and, after a minute of conversation, Asma would always excuse herself that she had to go. One day, after a long time, I called Seema Khala and when I told her I was in Islamabad she thought I was joking. She put down the phone and called home and confirmed of that from Asma. I called her two days later, but she never spoke. She refused to speak to me just like Aba. I never knew what were *her* reasons. I took the admission in Fine Arts and discovered that the number of girls in university was higher than boys. They were from different families and most of them came from small towns and villages. They said they didn't face difficulties from their parents, but their relatives had objections. Their obstacles were faced by their fathers who stood for their daughters. They would often ask me why my father never came and I would always make up an excuse. After six months I got the call from home that Aba was diagnosed with leukemia. I couldn't believe my ears, as he was healthy and fine a few months before. At the end of the week, after submitting my assignments, I left for Quetta. I went to Aba's room and I was shocked to see him. He was grown old and had lost so much weight that for once I thought there were just bones, on the bed. I sat on the bed and I couldn't control my tears. I held his hand and kissed it and placed it on my eyes. Tears started rolling down his cheeks too. He was dying and he knew that.

"I will be fine, won't I?" he asked like a child.

"Yes Aba you will," I assured him.

He looked at my clothes: I was wearing a simple black shirt with polka dots.

"You look just like your Ama."

I smiled and looked at my shirt.

"Go open that cupboard, there is an album, bring that," he pointed through his eyes. I went and brought the album. He asked me to turn the pages and show him the photos. On one page he asked me to stop,

"This. See, this in the corner. Your Ama is wearing a same dress." I looked at the black and white photo and smiled. She was wearing exactly the same print. I was astonished how Aba could remember this photo. *Did he see these photos many times?* I thought.

"Pari, how are your studies going? Did you pass or failed in your tests?"

I laughed and cried. "I got A in all subjects, Aba."

"*MashaAllah*, work hard and never give up."

"I won't," I promised.

Cancer had changed him from inside and out. He was no more roaring but speaking softly. *Allah, please, give him life. I want his love. Don't let him go!* I prayed.

I stayed there for two weeks and then my final exam date came. I had to go, I couldn't skip the exams, as I was on scholarship. I was in a dilemma. I never wanted to leave my dying father while, on the other side, university was my whole future. I decided to go, not because I was careerist, but I wanted to fulfill my promise I made to Aba. During two weeks Aba's condition had become critical; he had lost his physical power and had become dependent on Elias and Furqan. Before going to the railway station when I went to his room to bid him a good-bye, knowing that it would be the last, he was shocked to see me carrying the bag.

"Where are you going?" He asked in whispers.

"Aba, I have an exam. I will come back." I sat close to him.

"Leave me! You are selfish!" He turned his face away from me.

"Aba. Please. Listen. I have to go. Please, look at me."

He shut his eyes and never looked at me.

"Pari, you will miss the train."

I kept sitting there until Furqan called me.

I walked out slowly, staring back for one last time, but he didn't turn his face towards me.

He died after one week and left me with a lifetime guilt.

Sixteen

I never went back, as the guilt was unbearable and there was nothing left. Aba's will revealed that he handed over all his property and business in Elias's hands. Whether it was his love or rage, that remained a mystery. Soon, after a month from Aba's death, Elias sold out much of the land and eventually the business shut down. The house became entirely his property and Furqan had no option than to leave and find a place of his own.

With each passing day I stopped looking back at things and people that were no more mine. My only home was the hostel and my only family were the friends I made in the new city. Even though after long years of being in a small valley, it didn't take me long to become a confident person. I was outspoken and outgoing with a big circle of friends. I would often be surrounded by friends who would come to share their love-life problems. Listening to their problems surrounded me with love, peace and harmony. I actively participated in various competitions and became quite known on campus.

I met my first love at the university. We weren't class mates, he was my senior, but we both were the members of drama association at university. He was the lead actor of two of the plays in which I performed. Actually he was also in the panel of students who took my audition. I never knew that I, who had always been bold and un-womanish, was beautiful too. I would always dress up in jeans and hood with joggers, and just once, on annual dinners of college, I would borrow long skirts from my roommate and attend the party without any jewelry or even a lip gloss. I always thought that dressing up or putting make-up would not help anyone to fall in love with me. I don't remember if I ever analyzed myself in the mirror during those days. It only served the purpose to help me tie my hair in a ponytail.

When I joined university, I was already prepared to get ignored by men. So it wasn't hard to accept when boys would call me 'hey bro!' or 'wassup dude?'

I was good at debate and speech so I was quite known on campus. One day, I saw the poster in university's café for drama audition. I, along with my group, went to the auditorium to enjoy the auditions and tease the ones who stepped on stage. I sat in last row of the hall and started chattering and hooting. All in a sudden a tall silhouette from first row appeared and started walking towards where I was sitting. When he became visible, I saw a tall, smart guy with specs, and a smart stare in his eyes, standing close to me. His arrival shut my mouth for a second, but I consciously ignored him and passed another comment on a person at the stage. He stood in front of me, blocking my view to stage and said, "If you are so courageous, then step on stage."

"Pardon?" I pretended, as I didn't understand what he meant.

"Hah! Nice! So you are here just for entertainment. Prudent!" He said. That hurt my ego and I couldn't help lying, "Well, you are mistaken," I suddenly found myself overconfident and I kept lying, "I am here for the audition." My friends turned and looked at me surprisingly. *No I am not buddies, save me!* I said in my heart while meeting their stare.

"Well, then move to the stage *if* you *really* are here for the audition."

I never gave a chance to myself to think, and left the seat and trod towards the stage and made him follow me as if I was a hired actor and had won tremendous awards. Though, later my friends said that I deserved one, for that acting!

He handed over me few pages in which the description of a scene was written and asked me to go through it. I read the description of the scene and to my disappointment it was a tragic romantic one. A girl getting married, *of course* not with the one she loved. It was a typical Indian or Pakistani story. The girl met her lover for the last time and bade him a good bye. The dialogues were highly dramatic but well written. It was unlikely that a tom boy like me would suddenly perform such a painful romantic scene, but there was no way. I gave a short glance at the back row. I could hear my heart beating fast and I cleared my throat. I had no idea what was the background of the story. They didn't give me any explanation or a complete script. Since they were not professional dramatists, then I had no complaint. The panic was overtaking my confidence and I didn't like that. To get rid of it, I decided to give a quick performance and leave the hall. Anyway I was not there to *really* act, so a possible rejection would be no offence.

"I am ready!" I announced. I heard my group saying, *"woohoo"* in unison.

"Okay! Come on the stage, then!" The same tall guy announced like a boss.

I climbed three short stairs and walked on a faded red carpet spread on the stage and stood in the center.

"Rizwan will read the lines of a boy," I heard him saying.

I saw a guy rising from the panel and coming on the stage with some papers.

"All right. Start!"

And there I was. Rizwan uttered his dialogue of a boy complaining to a girl for betraying him and without any smile I started my dialogue.

"How can you think it was my decision?! Don't you know the society we live in?!The families we grow up in? If it was my decision, then you know who I would have tied a knot with!! I don't care how much money he has! I don't want his house or his name! I want you! I love you!!! And still you think it was my decision?! Life is all about decisions. Conscious and unconscious. Joyous and painful. But in this society a woman has not many decisions to take! We just decide the meals to be cooked three times a day... and sometimes those too aren't of our choice!!!"

More than a dialogue it was a monologue. But what surprised *me* was the applause from the audience. What surprised *him* were the tears in my eyes. I couldn't believe I did it so well. I really felt I was the girl who lost her love. I never had such experience, but I empathized with the character. Probably, deep down inside me, my soul knew I was a girl. My shabby jeans and boy cut was not enough to hide those sensitive and fragile emotions.

"You are in," that tall guy announced. "By the way I'm Amir."

"I'm Pari," I replied.

"Welcome to the club, Pari."

I smiled and wondered how he could select an unattractive girl for the leading role. As soon as I joined my group mates, they asked me for a treat. A few minutes later I was in a café spending all the bucks I had, knowing I would be fasting for the next week, at least.

We started the rehearsal right after the day of the audition. I would spend all my evenings in auditorium. Rehearsals never seemed a tiring job. Half of the time would end in laughter and teasing each other. There were students I never knew before and soon we became good friends. Every afternoon we would beg one fellow to get something from the café. Each one would make lame excuses and at the end it would be decided to go together. Our voices would fill the café's already-noise-polluted environment. Usually hostel residents would be there to have lunch as they never liked the food provided in mess. Once we would return to auditorium it usually took 30 minutes to get tuned into positions. After two scenes, when it got dark, everyone would ask to leave. Staying at university till late evening was a problem for girls, especially day scholars. I never had to worry, as I was living in the hostel. As soon as day scholars would start to leave, Amir used to get furious for not completing the rehearsal. Everyone would calm him down and took him easy while I always avoided talking to him for unknown reasons. When I look back I find that it was my ego which prevented me to talk to him. I wanted to be felt special and therefore I would try my best to ignore him.

Why Amir selected me was another riddle which got solved right after I read the complete script. The play was written and directed by Amir. The protagonist was a tom boy, too, who won the heart of her lover. She never tried to appear attractive, but somehow, boys couldn't help falling in love with her. Rizwan played the role of her lost lover. Probably, Amir found the girl's character in me. In half of the play I wore my normal boyish clothes, but later I had to dress in a typical Asian girl fashion. For that I had to borrow some from my friends. They brought me fancy *Shalwar kameez* and *sarees* along with their jewelry. They also provided me with makeup as they were too excited to see that other side of me. The day of the final rehearsal, just a day before the real show, all the actors had to wear their costumes. When the scene of the wedding came, I quickly changed into the red *lahnga* provided by my closest friend Maira. Tania, who was assigned as make-up artist, quickly did my make-up. She already had put the foundation on my face, so that saved time. She perfectly did my boy cut and with the jewelry she made it appear no more boyish. In those moments I hadn't much time to look at myself in the mirror. I was quickly sent to stage with my gown hiding my flat sandal. It was never easy to put high heels and I knew I would create a funny scene out of it. Eventually, everyone agreed and let me wear flat shoes knowingly that it wasn't a professional play which would be recorded or broadcast.

As I reached the stage I got absorbed in the performance. During the parting scene I had to hold Rizwan's hands. That day I saw a strange glow in his eyes, which I never saw during all rehearsals. When it was over I looked towards my team, who appeared amazed. I eyed Amir, but he seemed aloof. He wasn't looking at the stage and I had a feeling he was intentionally doing so.

I went back to the changing room and met Tania there. She was at her spirits.

"Everyone was stunned! What a change in you!" She said loudly.

I glanced in the mirror and found a different person standing there. I surely looked different. I was embarrassed to see so much artificial color on my face. But I never wanted to hurt Tania's feelings. As I knew that it was I, who wasn't used to all that make-up, so I replied, "You did a great job!"

"Did I?" She asked happily.

"I bet."

After I changed, I left the changing room and we all decided to skip the ritual of going to the café, for that day. We all thought we should take a good rest, before the next day. We needed to be fresh and active, as the real show would be more hectic, and going to café would mean spending two hours there in useless talks. It was always hard to leave. All that time Amir neither talked nor even bothered to give any instructions, which wasn't usual of him. That irritated me and made me uncomfortable.

The day later all the students dressed in their best outfits gathered in auditorium. The annual drama competition was one of their favorite entertainments. Every year different universities would come to our campus, but there would be a performance by five universities. Five plays and each shouldn't be for more than 30 minutes. Had it been more than half an hour, the judges would disqualify the team. As a host university, our university would always open the show. We were the first to perform. It all went well. Once again, to my team's surprise, I cried in the last scene and gave it a real touch. During all the rehearsals I never once felt any personal emotion when I touched Rizwan. But then the wedding-day scene and the parting scene, where two lovers meet for last time, came. I held Rizwan's hand and a strange emotion arouse in me. There was giddiness and an urge to hold him forever. Something was strange in him too. He held my hands tighter. He looked in my eyes as if he really loved me, and it wasn't a play but my real wedding. I guess everyone felt that too. There was pain in his voice, and his eyes got moist. Someone whistled from the audience and all hooted. Nothing moved Rizwan. Nothing moved me. Not once we got confused. He appeared as calm as he was among the crowd but not an actor on the stage. I completed my final line, *"I have to go! This is what is written for me. This is what is written for us. Forgive me!"*

We started walking backwards facing each other and our hands stretched in the air. The curtains were drawn. No doubt we got a huge applause at the end. And the judges, who were members of the provincial drama association, declared us winners. We screamed like kids. We jumped and hugged each other. We forgot that our culture prohibits physical closeness between persons of opposite sex. We didn't care, because in our heart we knew our families weren't watching us. It was a students' gathering and no family members were invited because of the less spacious auditorium. In that moment, we broke all the norms and rules. After a long hug we planned to go to McDonald's rather the university's café. I changed into my normal clothes, but didn't remove the makeup. Suddenly, Amir interrupted us, "You guys carry on. I have some work."

We all gave him a surprised expression.

"Work? Now?" Tania asked.

"Oh, dear director, now you are no more a boss! Come with us!" One of his friends said.

Everyone forced him and finally he climbed into his car. For the first time he turned to me and asked, "Who are you going with?" The question was quite sudden and honestly I hadn't decided yet. I looked around and suddenly Rizwan said, "She will come in my car," and turned towards me, "won't you?" I looked at Amir and before I could open my mouth he shrugged and looked at me like a mother who is trying to reprimand her kid in public without a word. He didn't wait for me to say something and drove the car with Aliya who had occupied the front seat. Amir left with three more friends at the back seat. I bade goodbye to my classmates and friends and told them I would definitely celebrate the day with them, too. Rizwan opened the front door of his car for me and shut it not too hard. He didn't ask anyone to join us and quickly drove away. We were almost twenty in a party and not more than six cars. Rizwan kept looking at me while driving and for the first time I felt nervous. I remember I blushed and he laughed. "What's so funny?" I asked.

"You are blushing!" He succinctly replied. And the more I blushed the more he laughed. There wasn't much traffic and soon our car was next to Amir's on red signal. He looked at me, but this time not like a mother, rather like a sad child. His expressions were so clear. He never tried to hide those as he would always. *Is he jealous?* My heart asked. *He doesn't love me,* my mind answered. *Who knows?* Was the heart's reply. But mind and heart were sure that something was *definitely* wrong. *Probably, Rizwan is flirting,* I thought.

Once we all reached McDonald's and settled on tables we asked two of us to place our order. They frowned at first, but finally stood in queue which luckily wasn't long. Once the order was ready, they called us to take the trays. While eating, suddenly one of Amir's friends and class mates, Musa, who acted as my father in the play, said to Rizwan, "Riz, when the audience hooted at that wedding scene I thought you would leave stage." Rizwan smiled. No reply. Amir didn't look up and kept dipping and rolling a French fry in ketchup.

"Were I you, I would have."

"Things done with passion don't let you stumble."

"Oooooh!" All said in unison.

"With passion or with heart?" Suddenly Amir asked.

"With love." It would have not shocked everyone if Rizwan hadn't said that while looking at me.

Amir's face color changed for a second and then, again, he concentrated on his fries. At least he tried to. At the same time, all my appetite was gone. Rizwan had made everyone curious. They started passing us strange smiles. It was clear they were looking at us as a couple. We all started to leave and this time Amir didn't ask me anything. He left as if I was not there.

Rizwan stood next to me all the time. This time everyone knew he would be going alone with me. They said bye and Tania winked at us. Once they left we went to car parking which was quiet and dark. Rizwan opened the door of his car for me and I got in without a word. My heart was beating fast and my hands were sweating. Rizwan took his seat, but didn't start the car. He held my hand and looked into my eyes. My heart was pounding fast and I didn't move back. This might gave him a signal that I was willing. He kissed on my forehead, nose and then, the next moment, our lips were twined. It was my first kiss. A kiss which is unforgettable. Sweet and soft, urging for more and more. But then he moved back, looked around and said, "Are you okay?"

I nodded.

He kept staring at me and then he hugged me. I hugged him back. I was under some trance. I wrapped his back. I tugged my lips on his neck, but let them closed. It was as if everything was happening because it was destined to happen. He rolled down my tee shirt from the shoulder and began kissing. We kissed on our lips for the second time. He held my face in his hands and tried to kiss me harder and that brought a pang of pain. It embarrassed me. I felt he wanted to satisfy himself. I don't know why, but I didn't like that thought. Slowly I moved back. Something bothered me: a feeling of guilt, perhaps. "Please drive me to the hostel," I said softly. "I will." He smiled and kissed my cheek. I didn't find that flirtatious, he had sincerity in those eyes. It took away my regret. I was in love.

Seventeen

I started seeing Rizwan after classes. Sometimes one had to wait for the other to finish off the class. He always seemed eager to see me. As soon as he would find me, his eyes would sparkle. He would always be reserved in public. I liked his consideration as that would save us from rumors, but everyone already knew we were dating. To avoid any physical gesture was compulsory, as our society would never approve that, no matter how much secrets they all had. But love doesn't see rules and norms. Love is wild and untamed. It is blind and stubborn. The attraction between Rizwan and me was powerful. We couldn't stop each other from all things which lovers do. Our meeting point was Rizwan's apartment. He was living with his friend, but whenever Riz took me there his friend wouldn't be there. Riz would say he would call before coming so I should be relaxed. One evening, when I was in Riz's arms, he suddenly started kissing me and next moment he took off my jumper. I was in trance, but then I felt he wanted to break the final rule: no sex before marriage. I sat up and quickly grabbed my jumper. He looked at me surprisingly then read my face for a minute. He understood that I wasn't happy.

"I'm sorry," he said and I felt he really meant it.

"Riz, you know it's not right. I know this all is not right. Still, *this* before marriage is impossible. We can't. We are Muslims!" I was in tears.

"Hey! Hey! I said I'm sorry. I won't do anything wrong. I promise."

"Marry me, then!" I suddenly said.

He was neither shocked nor surprised. He softly held my hand and said, "I will."

"When?" I was persistent.

"I will talk to my parents."

This satisfied me. "I have to go, now. It's late." And he stood up to drop me back.

After a week I asked him if he talked to his parents and what they said. To my surprise he said they refused to get him married until he would get a job and settle down. I told him that without a proper relation I wouldn't be seeing him because "my conscience keeps haunting me". He asked for some time. That day, to keep my word, I left the university without him. I knew if he had been with me then we would be physically close again. He insisted to drop me, but I replied, "Make this relation legal," and left.

The hostel was at fifteen minute walk. I was walking along the street, when suddenly a black Hyundai slowed down. It was Amir. "Come. I'll drop you."

"I am fine," I answered.

"Pari, don't be a fool! It's no more dusk. If you wanted to walk, then you should have left early."

I didn't like his opinion, but I slowly got into his car.

"So where is Riz? Doesn't he always drop you?" He asked without looking at me.

It was a fact that Riz always dropped me, but I never knew that he knew that. I asked foolishly, "How do you know?"

"Everyone knows."

"He wanted to, but he had to leave early. He had some work," I lied.

"I don't know if he would really marry you." That was the least thing I expected him to say.

"Pardon?" I couldn't hide my anger.

"Nothing. I just want you to make sure you have a secured future."

"I think you are getting personal. That's my matter."

"Listen, Pari! You aren't that strong as you appear. I don't want you to break in love!"

"What do you know about me? You know nothing!"

"I know you are a girl who can cry while acting."

"That was *acting!"*

"But life isn't. Think carefully."

"Why are you driving here? You know where the hostel is, don't you?" Suddenly I noticed we were on another street.

"I am saying something," he stressed on his each word.

"And I heard you! Please drop me, now!" I started getting worried, *what if Riz sees me? He would probably not like that I refused to go with him and took a lift from Amir.*

"I love you, Pari."

My jaws dropped and I was blank. I suddenly realized my mouth was dry. I couldn't say a word. "Stop the car!" It was the only thing I said.

"Listen!"

"Enough!" I stammered.

He didn't stop, but quickly drove me to hostel. As soon as I stepped out, I heard him saying, "I'm always here." I had already shut the door so I thought it was useless to reply. I ran inside the building.

I couldn't sleep all night. *Amir loves me?* I felt if I didn't tell that to Riz it would be kind of dishonesty on my part. Riz wasn't only my love but a closest friend too. Since he came in my life I stopped seeing many of my friends. I would share everything with Riz. He was a good listener and he never made me feel that he was bored in my company. I really wanted to call Riz and tell him what happened. I was in a dilemma. I kept questioning myself. *What if Amir tells Riz before I do? What if I tell Riz and he gets mad?* Whatever happened that evening had surely disturbed me, but there was a strange kind of happiness crawling inside me. Heart in heart I felt like a queen, for being loved by two men. I knew it wasn't right, but I couldn't help smiling on the thought that Amir, who apparently ignored me, was actually in love with me. I recalled the events of rehearsals and understood that during that time, more than being detached, Amir had been seriously envious.

Days went by and I never had the courage to tell Riz about that evening. I could recall Hardy's *Under the Greenwood Tree*, in which Fanny thought not to ever reveal her secret to her husband. I found it a sensible advice. Men can't understand all secrets, no matter if they are stereotypical like Aba or modern like Rizwan. There are few things which need to be hidden. Few moments which can never be explained, therefore, they leave a void behind. In fall, Riz submitted his research paper and went back to his city. It was at four hour drive from the capital. He promised he would convince his parents at least for our engagement. He knew the only person in my family to attend our wedding would be Furqan and convincing him wouldn't be a problem. All I had to do was to call and ask him to reach us. I knew my marriage wouldn't be like traditional weddings. All I longed for was a home and a family. All in sudden I tended to forget all my dreams about career and job: I just wanted to be with Riz. Riz hardly called after leaving for his hometown. I kept dropping him messages and said I understood as he certainly was busy with his family. One day, Furqan called me and we talked about random things and suddenly he switched the topic to my future plan. I did not know if it was a right time or not, but I told him about Rizwan. He was quiet for a moment; he, of course, was not ready to accept that his sister would have a love marriage. But, like an understanding brother, he asked me, "Do you see yourself happy with him, in the future?" I assured him I certainly did. He said he would visit me soon so he could meet Rizwan. He told me that I should not discuss the matter with any of our half siblings. I myself never wanted to. I knew they would never approve my marriage, like it happened about my education. I was more than happy. I was relaxed that Furqan, my only brother, had no issues with my love marriage. I texted Riz and I told him about my discussion with Furqan. It was the first time in a whole week that he replied promptly and that hurt me a little. He sent, "WHY???" with lot of question marks. I got uncomfortable and panicked on this reply. I called him immediately and he sounded uncanny. I asked him what was the matter and he said his mom was furious and she wouldn't approve our marriage at any cost.

"But you have to convince her! You know it's my last year at university. I can't go back!"

"I'm trying," he said displeasingly.

"Why are you talking like this? As if you didn't want to talk."

"I told you I'm bothered because of my mom."

I wasn't satisfied, but I changed the topic. After a few words he said he had to go. He hung up the call first. That was the first time ever, as before he had a ritual that, no matter what, I always had to disconnect the call. *Something has changed!* My mind screamed. I tried not to ponder over it.

After a couple days Riz called me and informed me that he was back. He was in the city to search a job. He talked to me like before and was eager to meet me. He picked me up after my class and headed to his apartment without asking me. When I noticed we were near his place, I reminded him again that it wasn't right to be alone. He suddenly got angry and said that I never missed him like he did. *"It's not true!"* I protested. "Well, then, don't think about anything." To assure him that I really missed him, I followed him to his apartment. As soon as he locked the door behind, we were in each others' arms, starting everything all over again. We lay down on a rug near the sofa and he stated moving his hands where he shouldn't. "Please. No. It's not right!" I protested lightly. He didn't seem to listen to me.

"Please stop", I said.

"I will marry you."

"When?" I asked.

"Next month."

"Really?"

He didn't answer and that day I lost the virginity. My conscience seemed to be asleep. There was no more regret or remorse. After all, he was my husband to be. I took a shower and dressed up. He was smiling and his eyes were sparkling. He was drenched in love.

"You are MY fairy!"

"And you are my elf."

"Elf?? Riz the Elf!" He laughed.

My phone rang and I quickly answered it. It was Furqan. He informed me that he would be in the city next morning. I turned to Riz and gave him this news with a grin.

"So you will be busy with your brother, hmm?"

"He is coming to meet you," I answered.

His face expression changed. He looked worried.

"What happened?" I was concerned.

"Nothing. I would love to meet him."

I didn't believe him.

Eighteen

Next morning I asked Riz to take me to the airport. He came on time and on my way he never once asked anything about Furqan. He was normal and calm. When Furqan came out we went to a nearby restaurant as it was almost lunch time. During the lunch no one mentioned anything about marriage. Furqan asked us to drop him to one of the hotels where he would be staying for a week. When we reached the hotel Furqan turned to Riz and said, "I think we should now talk about important things."

Riz remained silent. Furqan continued, "Now you both have decided to marry, I have no objection. It's your life and I don't want to interfere. I want you to marry before she leaves university as I'd be moving to Canada this year. She can't go back and you must know that. When can I see your parents?"

"They didn't agree," he said. I was as shocked at this reply as much as Furqan was.

"What do you mean? Are you saying you aren't willing to marry?!" Furqan was definitely furious.

"I don't mean to say I will not marry her. I want to. It's just that I have to marry her in court. I will disclose it to my family once things are right."

"And when will they be?" Furqan asked coldly.

"Not more than a year. Trust me." There was an urge in his voice which melted my heart.

"And where will she live during *this year?*"

"In my apartment. It's my own apartment. I am currently living there with my friend, but he will leave. He is just a paying guest."

Furqan stayed quiet and gave it a thought, and then he turned to me and said, "Well, things are on you, now, Pari."

I cleared my throat and then managed to say something sensible, "Bhai, you go and take rest. I'll see you in the evening."

He nodded and left the car quietly.

While on our drive back and after a long irritating silence, I turned to Rizwan, "Furqan is here for a week. Then he will leave for Karachi to finish his visa process."

"Hmm."

"'Hmm'? 'Hmm' is not the answer."

"I am listening."

"I *said* I want an answer! What are you up to?"

"I told you, right? I am ready to marry you in the court. It should be confidential."

"Shall we inform our close friends?"

"No. Not now. Don't want any problem."

"Are you happy?"

He looked at me and love reflected through his eyes, "Of course, sweetheart! I have no words to describe it!"

"I can see that." I smiled. I believed him.

In the evening I met Furqan and he asked me to arrange the marriage on Thursday as he had a flight on Monday. It was just a paper marriage so there was nothing to worry about the arrangement. Furqan promised to send me some money for a wedding gift once he would reach Canada. I understood his financial situation and had no complaints. I was glad that he was such a supportive brother, unlike my other siblings. Furqan asked me several times to think again about the marriage and I replied that there was no time to think. "It's all written." One day when I gave my usual answer, he couldn't resist.

"I know it's all written, but I don't want you to suffer like Ama."

"Riz isn't like Aba. He is a loving man and he isn't selfish like Aba."

"Don't call him selfish. He is a dead man now,"

"I don't know if you love or hate Aba." I sighed.

"I don't hate anyone. I just want you to be happy. I want you to live peacefully. We have had enough of bad times. Anyways, take this."

Furqan gave me some money to buy some decent clothes for myself. I had some saving from scholarship money, too. On that evening I went out with Maira to the nearest shopping mall and did some shopping. I pretended that Furqan had asked me to do some shopping for Sobia. Though she was my closest friend, there was so much of my life hidden from her. I always had been good at masquerade. Maira didn't question anything. She knew that in Quetta there weren't many big malls. More than clothes I purchased paintings and some home essentials. In my imagination I had shifted the paintings numberless times on the walls of Riz's apartment. When I came back I opened my journal after long time and wrote all I was feeling. Last time I had written something was almost two years back when I had felt lonely in the middle of night. It's strange that people stop communicating with their oldest and best friends when they find new people and new things to keep them happy. A kind of selfishness which we all hide inside our souls. My journal had always been my best friend, but when I had left Quetta and the new city had mesmerized me, I had stopped writing diaries. That day I was more than happy. A dream of my own home, a husband, children and a family, was about to come true. I imagined myself taking care of Rizwan every day. I took a vow to keep my marriage filled with love and utmost care, no matter how much I had to sacrifice. I promised myself that, no matter what, I would always stand by Riz. I took my journal and started writing,

Today it is a very special day for me! Yes! I have found my love! I know I have made a right decision in choosing this man. His chanting personality has mesmerized me, moreover it is not only I who loves him, but he loves me too. He loves me madly. What a woman needs on earth more than love, to survive, isn't that so? After two days he will be here to pick me. I am moving to his place, our wedding party will be after few months. He has to take care of few things. Oh, there is so much to tell you, my dear diary, about my elf! Yes, Elf, that is how I call him. Do you know what he calls me? Fairy! Though I am not one, but that is his love which makes me feel that I am a fairy. I have done all my shopping. I have been saving for long to be with him. I am going to start my life and this time nothing will go wrong. I know clouds have shed and now it's a bright sparkling day. Nothing in this world is permanent, all things are following a Divine rule and that is CHANGE. Few years back I thought life would never have changed, it was stuck, for me, I did not die, but I felt I was without soul. My soul was either lost, or I never possessed any, it's still to figure out, but now I do not intend to look back. He must be doing preparations too. I do not want to ever worry him in life. I am very happy and nothing in this world can make me sad any more. After all he is now all I have, and no one in this world can give me more happiness than him. I madly love him and of course he loves me the most!

I kept sitting with my diary for a half an hour, then I heard the noise from the corridor. Probably, some girls were going to get food from the mess. My appetite was lost. I wasn't hungry, so I decided to pack my things. Luckily, my roommate wasn't there. She had gone to her hometown for her sister's wedding. I was sure that she wouldn't be coming back before two weeks. I was glad that I did not have to face her stares. She definitely would have become curious if she had seen my shopping. I planned to submit a leave to the hostel warden. I decided to cancel my registration at the end of the month. Before wrapping the paintings, I took photos of them and I sent them to Rizwan with a message, "For our new home." He didn't reply. *"He must be busy."* It took me three hours to pack everything, from my books to my clothes. It was almost 11:00 PM and I lay down to sleep. But I couldn't sleep and I was eagerly waiting for Riz's message. I wanted to talk to him. I wanted to talk about future plans. No matter how many times we spoke about those things, I wanted to repeat them. It was ego or concern which stopped me from messaging him, so just to kill time I went online on Facebook. I was scrolling down that I suddenly noticed Riz was online. If he was online, he could have messaged me. I tried to think of sensible reasons. *He must be talking to some close friend. OR he must have come online to check his notifications.* I decided to stay unnoticed.

I didn't message him. Surprisingly, he too didn't notice I was online. That meant he was on chat, not on his page. *I don't want to think bad. I am happy, today!* I told myself. But I stayed online till 1:00 AM. Finally, sleep took over me and when I woke up it was ten in the morning. The first thing I checked was my phone. No message from Rizwan. Not a single call. I went online on Facebook and it showed *Active six hours ago.* "SIX hours ago"? It was enough to surprise me. He would never stay up so late. I decided to call him. He didn't answer. I went to the mess; I got the breakfast and ate a slice of bread. I called Furqan and told him that I would be meeting him around 4:00 PM. In the afternoon I called Riz again and he didn't answer. I dropped a message that I was waiting for him to pick me up so I could see Furqan. It was almost 4:00 PM and there was no call from Riz. I started getting worried. I thought to call any of his friends, Musa or Amir, who were usually with him in university. It could be they were with him. Before deciding whom to call, I went online again, on Facebook. What shocked me was that Riz was *Online.* I hated technology in that moment. I remembered that I had his Facebook password, but I tried to keep my patience. *I shouldn't spy on him*, I told myself. I took a cab and I went to see Furqan to his hotel. It was obvious from my face that something was bothering me. He asked me several times and I made an excuse that I had a restless night. He started to counsel me for the things which were last on my mind.

"I know it's not like a typical wedding. You stay strong. At the end what matters is your happiness. I am here and I am your family."

I nodded. We went out and walked to the nearest café. He kept telling me about his new job and things to be done in short time. While listening to him, I held my phone tightly on a hope to get a call or message from Riz.

When it was almost seven in the evening I told Furqan that I would leave and would see him next day.

"Isn't Rizwan going to see us?"

"No, he is busy. He is setting up the apartment," I lied.

"I was hoping to have a dinner with both of you together. All right, see you tomorrow, then."

I was quite astonished that not once Riz texted me. When I reached my hostel room, I took my phone and called him. He didn't answer. I left a message that it was important. I kept waiting for a reply until I slept.

Next morning, I checked my phone as soon as I woke up. *Something is seriously wrong,* I thought. My palms started sweating and I could hear my heartbeat. He *didn't* message or call. I couldn't control my anxiety, so I continued calling Riz. After calling him almost ten times I messaged him and pledged him to reply.

"Please message or call."

He finally called me in the afternoon and I quickly answered the call.

"Thank God you called! Where were you?"

"Just here," he replied casually.

"What do you mean, *'here'*? You know that we are getting married tomorrow! Right?"

"Hmm."

"'Hmm'?? What's wrong?!" I freaked out.

"I want to tell you something."

"What?" My heart started beating fast.

"Why don't you go to Canada with Furqan?" He said normally.

"What? And are you telling or asking? What's wrong?"

"I can't marry you."

I was silent. It was like my spinal cord refused to send stimuli to my brain. I shook my head and laughed.

"Stop joking. Okay, tell me, how are you?"

"I'm not joking. I can't marry you."

"What do you mean? Is it because of your mom?"

"No."

"Then?"

"I don't know."

"YOU DON'T KNOW?! DO YOU KNOW WHAT YOU'RE SAYING?!"

"Listen Pari! Don't waste your life for me. Go with Furqan."

"Riz!!! We're marrying tomorrow! Right?" I noticed tears rolling down my cheek. I shut my eyes and prayed silently *No God! Please, no more pain!*

"Pari, I told you. I can't. Means I can't." This time there was a command in his voice.

He didn't seem to be in a mood, but finally I convinced him. He asked me to wait for half an hour. Those were the most longest and painful thirty minutes of my life. I didn't know what to do. I had no idea what would happen next. I kept telling myself that Riz must be concerned about his parents. But somehow my mind would question *What if he really leaves me?* I didn't know. I had no idea. After 45 minutes he arrived. I asked if we would go to his apartment, but he said that his roommate was there. We parked the car in nearest park's parking.

"What's wrong?" I asked with shaking voice.

"I can't marry you."

"You already told me this. What happened, suddenly?"

"I don't know."

"Tell me!! What shall I say to Furqan?"

"Anything."

"What, *anything?*"

"I don't know," he replied indifferently.

I cried and couldn't stop shaking. I never saw him so aloof and detached. He was calmly sitting and playing with paper, pen and sometimes steering. I grabbed his hand. This time I took his hand in my both hands and pleaded like a person pleading for their own life before being executed.

"Please, tell me."

"I said I can't marry you."

"Then why did you ask me to marry you?"

"I don't know."

My mouth was dry and my shoulders were heavy. I had no words and no energy to beg him. I hugged my knees. That moment surrounded by chanting birds and crackles of children, I was all alone in darkness. I was no more with the person I used to know, but with a stranger on an unfamiliar land.

Without asking me he started the engine and drove me back. I kept looking at him and he didn't stare at me for once. I quietly left his car. I had no words. I wasn't given any explanation. All in sudden the person whom I considered my protector made me feel so vulnerable. Life never changes; it's our way of looking at it, changes. I came to my room and looked at all the packed bags. Where was I? Who should I call? Suddenly I realized how lonely I was. Since Riz had come in my life, he had become my only friend. With him I had lost my best friend. I had no one to talk to. I had no shoulder to cry on. I never wanted to tell this to Furqan because I had no patience to hear *I told you. Think again.* At heartbreaks we don't need a reminder that we made a mistake, but someone who just lets us soak their bosom. I kept sitting in same position for more than two hours when I heard the phone ring. It was Furqan. Of course he was waiting for me and I was supposed to meet him. I cancelled his call. I needed time to think what to tell Furqan. I was still certain that Riz must be helpless. He must be in some big trouble. With this thought I dialed his roommate, Asif's number. After few rings he answered and spoke cheerfully, "Hey, Pari!"

"Hello, Asif," I tried to sound normal.

"Where have you been?"

"I'm here only. Busy with projects and all."

"Yeah. Your last year at uni! I miss that period, man!"

"Man"? He will never change, I thought.

"I understand. Well, Asif, are you with Rizwan, right now?"

"No. I am not. I'm not in Islamabad. I left his apartment after submitting my research paper."

And that was news to me, because Rizwan would never mentioned that; he rather told that he was still there.

"Ah. Okay. So if you come, then do meet me."

"Yah, sure! Is everything ok? Aren't you in touch with Rizwan?"

"Yeah. Everything is fine. He wasn't answering, so I thought you probably know."

"Didn't he tell you I don't live there anymore?"

"I guess he did. I just forgot," I tried to sound normal.

After I hung up the call I sat in same position and kept staring at the wall. I had no idea what to do. I needed an explanation. We humans are strange; we accept the fate simultaneously, if the reasons are clear, but the same fate is unacceptable if we are left without an explanation. We crave for it and never let our wounds close. My wounds turned open before they were closed.

I held my phone and went on the phone book. I never had to scroll down till R to dial Riz's number, it was always on the top. I had added his number with asterisk before R, *Rizwan*. The more I looked at his number, the more I cried. I wanted to hear his voice. I wanted to hear all those promises he ever made.

I went online on Facebook and found he was online. *What the hell!! How can he be so calm?* Finally, I logged off from my account and logged in from his. Thankfully he hadn't turned on the privacy alert, so he didn't get any notification of my log-in. I went to his messages and my only intention was that to see when he sent the last message. I never knew I would discover a new chapter. The last person whom he sent a message was some girl with name Sania. She sent the message a second before and Riz was online and chatting to her only. I scrolled up their conversation and found they seemed to be in love. Riz had made same promises of marriage to her. They were exchanging notes of love with each other. I didn't blink. I found the reason and I wish I never had. It was the sheer pain. A pain of sudden betrayal tore me apart. I took my bag and left the hostel. After 10 minutes I was in cab on my way to Riz's apartment. Why? I never knew. I reached where he lived and slowly started climbing the stairs of that five stories building. Once I reached the front door of his apartment, on the third floor, I slowly knocked the door. I was sure he never expected me to be there alone. He knew I was a coward who would never go out alone. I knocked the door harder and a moment later I heard his footsteps.

"Coming!" He cheerfully said.

He opened the door and turned blank from seeing me. After few seconds he screamed, "Why are you here? Don't you understand I told you not to contact me?"

I was no more astonished. A man who can cheat can forget to show gentleness too. I no more expected him to be kind. I knew he wanted to get rid of me. I was broken, but I wanted to take out all my frustration. I pushed him aside and entered.

"Asif is inside! Don't create a scene!"

Asif? Hah! I looked around and found his laptop on the sofa. I quickly grabbed it and saw he was on Facebook.

"What are you doing?" He shouted.

"To help you!"

"Are you nuts?"

"I was! But no more!"

I opened up his inbox and turned the screen towards him.

"Here! Here it is! I asked you why you can't marry me and you said you don't know! Right? So I'll make it easy for you! Just say,-Pari, I can't marry you because I have found someone to flirt with! Someone who won't bring her brother to marry her, because it's easy to get rid of someone who lives in virtual world –!"

"Listen! Pari! She is just a friend!"

"'Friend'? Enough of your lies! Enough!"

I walked out and he ran after me. He grabbed me and tried to kiss my lips. I pushed him back and started to walk out. But then I turned, walked close to him and stared at him. As soon as he extended his arms to hold me, I slapped him as hard as I could on his face.

"What a disgusting soul you are!" I grabbed him from his shirt and almost lost my senses and screamed, "Why? Why me?! I loved you! With all of my heart! All of my soul! Tell me what you need! Do you want me to wait for months, years or decades? Tell me!! I will wait! But why did you cheat? Leave her and I swear I will never complain for what you did! We will have our family! Yours and mine! Please don't do that!"

And I broke again. I started begging him once again. He immediately turned into an animal. He put his hand on my mouth and warned me not to make a noise. He was concerned about his image, about his dignity. He pushed me out of his apartment and shut the door. I slowly dragged myself out and made my way out of the building. I sat down on the footpath and I put my head in my lap. It wasn't safe, for me, to be out at that moment. I was in a society where chaste girls never step out at that hour. But I was not chaste. I had lost my dignity, my purity, in the hands of that man, and, there I was, under the sky, unprotected. Sitting there made me clearly see the real face of Rizwan. I understood that he had tried to convince me of his loyalty because he couldn't see me strong. As soon as I had been at his feet, the animal inside him had been satisfied. How good he was, as long as he needed me, or probably my love made me see the goodness only. The blindfold was undone and the mask of his sincerity was gone. Furqan was continuously calling. He certainly wanted to know about going to the court. I had no answer and no strength. I texted him that Rizwan left for his town as his dad had had a heart attack. I typed and retyped the message several times. It was hard to lie. To this day, I never understood why for some people it's so easy to lie, while others never find the heart to. Furqan called me as soon as the message was delivered, but I cancelled the call. I stood up and started walking along the road. There was no cab and a fear invaded me. The thought of being so vulnerable made me cry again. It was the first time I was out alone after the sunset. I was walking with my head down and tears were rolling down my cheek, when suddenly I heard the honk. My heart jumped and without looking up I started walking faster. The car stopped close to me and I realized someone was following me. I forgot the pain of the betrayal and I got concerned about my safety. I started to run.

Nineteen

I heard someone calling my name. It was a familiar voice from the past. I turned around and found Amir was taking big steps towards me. I stopped and dropped, like a ball, on my feet and started to cry. He ran and held me from shoulders.

"Pari! What happened? Relax. Shh, don't get scared. I'm so sorry, I didn't mean to scare you."

I couldn't breathe. I couldn't say a word.

"I saw you alone and I got worried," he tried to sooth me.

I was sobbing like a child. I stood up and followed him to his car. He gave me water and tissues. He kept looking at me till I stopped crying. Once I relaxed he started again, "Tell me. What happened? What are you doing near Rizwan's apartment at this hour, where is he?"

"He's in his most perfect world, with the most perfect people."

"Tell me, what's wrong?"

With tears and stammers I narrated everything. He didn't interrupt or said something, but his face expressions kept on changing. He seemed shocked and surprised. Once I finished he looked at me and started, "Pari, I never knew that you were in a relation with Riz, after that play. I had an idea that you both were together, but all of us would often say that Pari is wise; she will understand the true nature of Riz and leave."

"Understand, what?"

"Don't you know he was always flirting with every girl at the university?

He never took any relation seriously. He lacks consistency and value for relations."

"Why I never noticed that? Why I never heard of it? Why you never told me this?"

"I tried, Pari, but you were always so rude to me. You hated me and I never knew why."

"I didn't. I mean, I never hated you. I was not comfortable after what you said. I thought it was kind of betraying Riz -" and as soon as I said that, I couldn't continue.

"I guessed you were in a relation with Riz, and I said that either at the wrong time or too late."

"You were in relation." This phrase hurt. I felt my chest tightened, it was like the ribs had collapsed on my tiny little heart. There I was again in tears.

"Hey! What happened?"

"If I had met you yesterday I would have said I *am* in relation with Riz, but you see, he has thrown me out like garbage."

"Don't say that! Don't use such words for yourself. You know who you are. It is he, who has lost you."

"After all break ups we are told the same thing by our closed ones that it's *them* who lost us," I said.

"I mean it. Trust me, he will get it back."

"But that won't do any good to me."

"You will forget, eventually. Let me drop you back home."

"Take me to Jinnah Avenue."

"Why? I mean..."

"I have to see Furqan, my brother. He is staying in Crown Plaza."

"Okay. And listen, I am always here. Just call me."

His words never touched me. They never reached me.

We didn't speak all the way and once I reached the hotel I got out and bent a little, "Thank you." I could hardly smile.

"Do you want me to wait for you?"

"No. I'll probably stay here."

"All right. That's a good idea. You need to be with someone."

"Bye."

"Take care."

I went inside and called Furqan. He answered on the second ring as he was holding the phone.

"I'm downstairs. What's your room number?"

"I'll come. You wait there."

He sounded as he didn't want me to go into his room.

He showed up in five minutes.

"Why are you here at this time," he studied my face and then continued, "what's happened?"

"I just came to see you. I thought to spend some time with you."

"That's good, but what happened? Has Rizwan left already?"

"Yeah." I didn't understand, was he asking me about leaving me or leaving Islamabad.

"Well, don't worry."

"Are we going to stand here and talk all this?"

"Let's go out and find some place to sit."

"Can't we go to your room? "

"Are you in your senses? What people would say?"

"Which people?" I looked around.

"It doesn't look appropriate,"

"I'm your sister!"

"They don't know."

"Why on earth they need to know?!"

He started walking out of the lobby and I followed him. Once we were out he turned to me.

"You know well, you know the mentality of people. I don't even appreciate that you're visiting me here at this hour."

And I lost all my patience. "Why are you so concerned about people?

Why can't you just focus on the relation which we have? Why have you always been ashamed of me? Why are you so much conservative?"

"It's not about being conservative."

"It has always been about men in my family! No one asked what I needed! No one bothered to show some love and see, here I am, destroyed, because the only man who showed me love has ditched me! Because no one showed me love before! If there had been any love, I would have differentiated between true and fake!"

My mouth was dry. My voice was hoarse. I was too tired to stand.

"Ditched you? What has he done?!"

"Nothing. He just left. He can't marry me and he never wanted to marry me."

I started to walk.

"Pari, listen. See, I told you to think again."

And that was the only thing I was afraid to hear.

"I know. It's all my fault. Let me take all the blame. Let me face this alone." Seeing me yelling at public place Furqan got embarrassed. He started to look around,

"Calm down. Don't shout here. Go to hostel and I'll see you tomorrow. Shall I get you cab?

And I started to walk out from the hotel without answering him back. After coming out of the hotel's street I looked around me and wondered what to do. There were no chances of getting a cab at that moment. My own people didn't seem to show any concern. It's strange that we are more concerned about the world, than about the ones living with us. I stared around and heard the barks of strayed dogs. I heard the voice of Amir in my head, *"call me"*, so I took out my phone and called Amir. "Are you nearby?"

"Hi!" I realised I asked without any "hello". I stayed quiet.

"Yes, I am near the hotel. Well, I'll come. Shall I?"

Without thinking I answered, "Yes", and then I told him where I was standing. Five minutes later he was there. I guess he looked around in a hope to see Furqan.

"Are you alone?" There was anger in his voice. Which showed how concerned he was .*Pari, don't judge. You are such a loser in human psychology, sociology, behaviour and everything.*

"I was with-" I couldn't think of what to say.

"Come inside." I got in the car and asked him to drop me at the hostel.

"I will. But will you be okay?"

"Why?"

"I mean, you are upset and it's not the right time to be alone."

"It's not a problem."

"What?" he looked surprised.

"Being alone."

"You look so different from the girl who acted in my play."

"That was a play. This is real life."

He didn't say anything. After reaching to the hostel he turned to me, "Go and sleep now. Don't stay up late. Have you eaten dinner?"

"Yes," I lied, and realized that I hadn't eaten since the morning. I walked inside and this time without any thanks or goodbye.

I fell on my bunk and closed my eyes. Tears rolled down my cheeks and I held my head in my hands. I eventually slept.

Twenty

Days kept running. Time never stopped and I kept living and kept breathing. Furqan left for Karachi and mentioned that his documents were almost ready. Amir kept contacting me during that time, but I confined myself in my own world. My classes were over and I only had to submit research papers. My only visits were to libraries or to a professor's office. My circle of friends, which had become smaller when I was with Riz, totally disappeared. Eventually I had no one to see or meet. My group mates, observing my mood, stopped calling me. I never called Riz again and he blocked me, not only from his life, but from all social accounts. I made a fake ID and would spy on him. It gave me a strange satisfaction to see him; even the strings of pain would not bother me. I enjoyed my affiliation with that pain. My pain became my souvenir, which kept reminding me what a fool I was.

One day, I was coming in the library and started reading the newspaper. Those days I would read the job vacancy column every day. A vacancy for an art teacher caught my eye. I jotted down the email address in my note pad where already several were written. Every afternoon I would go to the computer lab before going to my room and send my CV to all the addresses.

I completed my graduation with all straight A's except for one B in History of Art and Civilization. I was confident that a bright future was waiting for me. *Everything will be fine,* I kept telling myself. I got the call from one of the known schools and got the job as an art teacher for O-level students. The salary wasn't much, but it was enough to pay my rent. I rented a room in a private hostel and I didn't take the mess service. I never had a breakfast and in the afternoon I would eat from the school's canteen. I never had time to cook, so I would usually spread mayonnaise on a slice of bread for dinner. Slowly, I started losing weight, but was moving on without knowing my destiny, without dreams. I would never visit parks or family places. It always hurt to see families, when you are alone in the world, when you have no home. It isn't about being jealous or insecure. It's something you can't help. I started taking tuitions for some other subjects, so I could sleep as soon as I hit the bed. I was running from my own mind that would not let me at peace. It was with me 24/7 and getting rid of it was not possible.

Furqan and Amir stayed in touch with me. Though I would not share much with them, because I had accepted that my problems were my possessions and I should keep them with me only. It was after six months since I started working when Amir called me. He insisted to see me. I refused as usual, making an excuse of being too busy, but he was persistent. Finally I agreed to see him at lunch. I would have never gone out with him at dinner, because I didn't want to give him any wrong inkling that I was in need of a masculine support. We met on Sunday afternoon and went to Diva. It was one of the finest eating places in Rawalpindi- a twin city of Islamabad. Although it was inside the public park, still it wasn't overcrowded at lunch time. We took the table in the corner and I immediately told Amir that I was not good at ordering food, so it would be better if he could order for me as well. He insisted that I should see the menu, but I closed that and started staring at the people around me. He ordered *palak paneer,* spinach with cheese, along with chicken steak, salad and *nans.* While ordering he looked at me and said, "At least choose the drink."

I saw that the waiter started to smile too.

"Lemon with mint will be fine."

Few minutes later the drinks were served. Amir started the conversation. He told me about his work and the busy schedule he had. He asked me about my job.

"It's okay, I mean, fine. But you know that in Pakistan girls who are living alone in private hostels are considered as easily available girlfriends. Either a man is in his 50's or 20's, he would always think we have no character and no respect."

"I understand, but you should not worry about people."

"I am not. I am least bothered, but this society respects females as wives, sisters and mothers only."

"And daughters, too."

"Yeah. Right. Only if she lives with her father."

"Why don't you apply in the university so you can have better opportunities?"

"I'm an art teacher. Here an artist doesn't make money, how can I?"

"But lecturers do get a good pay."

"Yeah. Only if they teach scientific subjects. The rest of us with degrees in art and literature burn their certificates."

"What was your CGPA?

"3.8. Straight As and one B."

"Incredible! That is such a worthy score for an Artist!"

"But still I'm just a teacher who has to take extra classes to make some bucks."

"That's just a beginning. Why don't you give me your CV? I'll ask my professors to help out."

"No. I don't need that now. Thank you anyway."

"Why?"

"I am going to Dubai."

"Dubai? When? Why? Who is there?"

I laughed after long time. "Wow, so many questions. Take a break! There's no one over there, but opportunities."

"Alone? And what do you know about Dubai?"

"Nothing. Everything has its first time and then nothing remains unfamiliar."

"It's not that simple and easy!" He was furious.

"Nothing is simple. Nothing is complicated. It's our way of looking at things."

"How will you cover the expense? Where will you stay?"

"Everything will be done at its right time."

"When are you leaving?"

"Next month."

"What? And you didn't even bother to tell me!"

"I told you now. In fact you are the first one to know."

"Only because I forced you to see me!"

We stayed quiet for a while and I kept playing with the cucumber in my plate. I wasn't hungry. I never was hungry those days. Food never tempted me.

"I wanted to say something," Amir looked at me thoughtfully.

"What is it?" I asked without looking at him.

"I want to marry you."

I smiled, "That's not possible."

"I can wait. Come back from Dubai and then we can."

"Don't wait for me, Amir. I am not coming back. I am setting all the boats on fire once I reach there."

"Who are you running away from? From Riz? Who is happy with his life?" He got louder.

I looked around and thankfully there was no one nearby, "Relax. I am not running from him. I just need my own space."

"I will wait."

"Don't."

For the rest of the evening we both stayed quiet. Just before dropping me, he said, "Before leaving for Dubai, let me know. I request. I will drop you to the airport."

I nodded. I was no more used to farewell words.

A month later I left for Dubai, with high hopes for an unknown destiny.

PART TWO

FAIZ

Twenty-one

I step inside the house hoping to see the lady whom this old man just called.

"Come inside. Leave your luggage here. Go and sit there. *Baaji* will be coming in a moment," he points towards the sofa, in a lounge which is just next to the entrance, after a small corridor. I leave my bags there. A shoulder bag with my iPad and other essentials and a trolley bag with clothes and some presents I bought for her. As usual I had no time to go for shopping so I bought some books for her from the airport. I know she adores books and choosing books is not even a problem. Give her anything and she will read. Few minutes later a girl, around twenty to twenty-five years old, comes from upstairs. I get baffled, but I stand up in courtesy.

"*Salam,* Greetings," I say.

"*Walikum Salam.*Faiz, I am Hoor. Your *Baaji's* niece," she speaks softly with a dim smile.

"Where is she?" I ask impatiently.

This time she doesn't smile, "She has slept early as she had taken the medicine. She will see you in the morning. Why don't you get fresh, and we can have a dinner."

"Slept"? I am shocked to hear that. She would wait for me for hours, to see me. She would cancel all her appointments, the day I would go to see her. How can she sleep without meeting me? I clear my throat, "Well, I am not hungry. I will just sleep, then."

"Alright then, Shafi baba will show your room. What would you like to drink, a tea or coffee?" She asks politely.

"Nothing. I won't be able to sleep then."

"Probably you will need something to keep you up."

"Why?" I smile.

"Wait a minute." She disappears in the room opposite to the lounge. She emerges after few seconds with a box in her hands. "She gave me this, before sleeping. She wants you to go through this before the morning."

I am definitely confused and she can read that very well. I take the box from her hands hesitantly, "What is this?"

"Well, see by yourself, when you go to your room." She gives me plain looks.

After few minutes Shafi Baba, the man who opened the door to me, comes and asks me to follow him upstairs. I look around in the hope to see someone, but all the doors are closed. *In which room she could be?* I ask myself. I really want to ask Shafi Baba, but I can't. I go upstairs and there are three rooms in a row. He opens the door of the first room. I go inside and see my bags on the maroon Iranian carpet spread on the floor. There is a single bed in the corner of the room and a writing desk opposite to it. There isn't much furniture. "A closet is in the dressing room," Shafi Baba says, then he opens the door and shows me: it is attached to the bathroom. "If you need anything, just ring the intercom." He points towards the intercom which is next to the entrance door.

"Thank you," I reply. I see the water bottle on the nightstand and realise there is nothing I might need tonight. Once Shafi Baba leaves, I put the box I am carrying on the bed. It is a beautiful wooden box but not too heavy. I really want to sleep, but then, out of curiosity, I open the box without even washing my face or changing my clothes. I find a framed photograph of me. It is my photograph in uniform, when I passed out from the aviation college. I was twenty-three year old, back then. I smile and keep the frame aside. There is a mug with *Baaji*'s photographs on it, I remember I gave this to her on her birthday. *Why has she given me this back?* I am a little upset. Then there is a photograph of her and her husband, and a black and white photo of her mom. She showed me that, once, and I immediately recognize her. There is one old paper and when I open it I smile again: it is the letter I wrote to her. My first letter. *But why has she returned these things?*

There is one leather diary in the box, but on top of that there is an old copy of a book by Mitch Albom, *For One More Day.* I open the book and find a note penned on the first page of the book, *For Faiz.* There is nothing more written under it. I flip through its pages and there is no paper or note inside. I keep it aside and take the journal out. I open the first page where there are four photographs pasted on the first page, two men out of one is I think of her husband, the one is probably of her brother I saw his photo years back, too. The other two are of her mother and one is mine. On the top of the photos it is written, *My World.* I smile for a moment, but a sense of guilt overcomes me. All this time I kept thinking that she hated me. I turn the page and start to read,

Story telling is a strange creation; it soothes us and sometimes plays skilfully with our emotions. It slowly rips up the delicate cores of our

heart which no one has ever touched. For an instant we forget that we are enjoying the reflection of our own self in the dancing phonemes of a story, the image which we hide from our souls. By climbing each part of a story we whisper, "yes, it is me! Oh, yes, it is so me.."

I stop for a while. I read the events which she had already told me years ago. I remember it was I who insisted to her to share everything with me. She only showed me the surface of the events, but the intensity of her pain, I can feel it just today. I can't determine when she wrote this journal. There is no fresh smell of the paper, but the pages haven't lost the colour, though the ink is a little faded. *Maybe she has finished it a month ago and then called me.*

I have been sitting in the same position since I started reading. I am disappointed that I didn't ask for tea. Hoor was right; I would be needing coffee to keep myself up. Actually, I need coffee to get rid of the fatigue. Now I am no sleepier, as I want to finish each page of this journal tonight. Tomorrow, early morning I'll see her and will tell her all that happened in these twenty-five years. I am sorry for not contacting her, though I always thought she should have contacted me. *Yet I should have contacted her. I'll apologize in the morning and this time when I go back I'll build the contact between her and Saba. I have photos of Saba and the children in my phone. I'll show them to her. She would be so happy to see me settled and successful!* I am talking to myself in head. I change the clothes and continue to read the journal.

PARI

Twenty-two

I had been saving the money since I had started the job. I went to the travel agency and applied for one month visit visa. Once everything was arranged, I called my first cousin who was married and settled in Dubai. I was only in touch with her through Facebook. I never called her earlier, because I knew that the first thing I would hear would be that I shouldn't go to Dubai as there are least chances to get a job. I messaged her on and once she replied I told her that I would be visiting Dubai. She told me that she would love to meet me, but when I mentioned that I needed her to keep me for a week in her house she was silent and never replied again. My brain didn't take long to register that, as I was quite expecting it. I kept wondering who to contact next and then I recalled one of my professors, who had always supported me. I called him and told him my situation and asked if he knew someone who could give me a place in their house. He told me that he would call me in half an hour. I thought he might not call, but then, again, I had no complain if he wouldn't. After ten minutes he called and told me that he had spoken o his sister who lives in Sharjah, which is next to Dubai, and would be happy to have me as long as I wished. I was in tears, "I don't know how to thank you, Sir! How shall I ever pay you back?" I asked while sobbing.

"Don't cry, my child! Just be successful and that's enough to pay me back! And yes, keep some room in your luggage. I'll send something for my sister, otherwise she will be crying on your shoulder. She is quite sentimental. You be careful!"

I laughed and I told him that I would carry anything. That day I learnt that blood is not always thicker. I got help from a person who shared no family ties with me. He was my spiritual father, though not too old, but proved to me that the world is not such a bad place to live.

As per the arrangement, Amir dropped me to the airport and my professor's sister was there to come to pick me up. It was the first flight of my life and I could feel the goose bumps. I was startled to see the giant iron bird to the naked eye. I had always waved the planes, as a child, but as an adult also I always wanted to see one. It was a dream lost in my unconscious, which came true that day. Since getting aboard till sitting down in the plane, I was looking around at everything. I was so much impressed with the Islamabad International Airport and never knew that more was yet to come. I got the seat next to the window and was more than excited. It was almost two hours of flight from Islamabad to the Shajah Airport. I almost forgot to blink my eyes when the plane started to take off. *I'm in the sky!* I was happy like a three-year-old kid. I am sure I couldn't hide my expressions well and gave everyone a hint that it was my first travel by plane! When it started to land, I looked out of the window and I could see a long road in the middle of the desert and I couldn't stop admiring the human mind for being so intelligent. Once the plane landed, I got a mixed feeling of loneliness and excitement. The loneliness, probably because I craved for a family, and the excitement, was that to explore that new world. I couldn't hold my surprise when I never had to climb down the stairs of the plane and catch the bus like I did in Islamabad. The plane door was joined with the airport through a tunnel and I kept walking, expecting to see the sky over my head, once out of it, but I was surprised to discover that I was already inside the airport. I started following the crowd and at that moment I recalled Bapsi Sidwa's novel, about a girl travelling to the United States for first time. I was exactly behaving in the same dumb manner. The Sharjah's Airport was far bigger than Islamabad's. The scintillating interior and designs captivated my eyes. After the eye scan I collected my luggage, but only after observing several people. Once my bag arrived I put it on a trolley and looked around for a crowd to follow. I had no courage to ask or talk to anyone, as they were from all over the world, and I found my confidence was gone. I saw a person in white shirt with the word SECURITY written on his front pocket. I went to him and started to talk in English, but he quickly switched to Urdu. He probably recognized my nationality from my dress.

"Do I need to get anything done or that's it?"

While looking at my luggage he said, "You got your luggage, so now you can go out through this way." He pointed towards a glass door. As soon as I came out, the hot wind welcomed me and I could taste the sand of grains in my mouth. I stared looking around and suddenly saw a lady in *shalwar kameez* looking right at me. She walked towards me and asked, "Pari?"

"Yes. Amna?" I said with forceful grin.

She hugged me and took the bag from my hands.

"It's okay," I insisted.

"Come on. We will rush to a car, before we turn into statues of sand!"

We got into the car and I noticed a man sitting on the driver's seat. She introduced us to each other. He was Amna's husband. He greeted me politely and then he told they had to pick their children from school on their way back home. I asked about her children and she told they have a boy who is seventeen and a girl of fourteen. I was quite uncomfortable and was continuously feeling that I'd be a burden on the family. Amna probably realized that and she started to tell me how happy she was to have me at her home. I was fighting back with my tears and kept nodding and smiling. A sense of homelessness and helplessness overcame me and I was reflecting a true example of self-pitying. We went to the school and I kept looking out of the window pane all that time. I was observing each and everything like a person who visits a city for the first time. Amna's husband Saad went out to get the children and soon he returned with an energetic boy and a lovely girl. Amna introduced me to them, "Pari, he is Basit and she is Lamya, and, kids, she is Pari Khala."

"Pari Khala, like a fairy?!"

And I was paralyzed, for a moment. Rizwan's voice echoed in my ears, *"You are my fairy."* I brought myself back from the past and tried to smile. I was happy they both greeted me warmly and called me *Khala,* Aunt. I smiled and looked at Amna and she cheerfully said, "I don't have a sister and my children would always wish they had an aunt whom they can complain to about me."

"Well, they have one, now," I said and in my heart I prayed that all that love and warmth they showed would stay with me forever.

We entered in an area where there were only buildings and I looked up."They are so tall!", I said quite loudly. And Basit quickly said, "When you will see the skyscrapers in Dubai, you will forget the ones here."

"Really?" I smiled.

"Papa said we will show you Dubai, this weekend!" Lamya was high at spirits. No matter how early children get up for school and hate studies, if they have a loving family they never seem to be tired once they are back home. The love of their family is reflected on their face.

Amna's apartment was on the fifth floor and it had a hall and two bedrooms. Unlike in Pakistan, there the majority of the population of Emirates lives in apartments. There are residential areas with villas but often too big and too expensive for small families. I was accommodated in a children's room which was divided with a cardboard partition, thus providing Basit and Lamya with their own rooms.

"I am sorry, you will be uncomfortable, as Lamya's room is quite small."

"No, it's okay. I worry I might disturb her privacy."

"No, she would be more than happy. You have no idea what a chatter box she is!"

Amna was right: not only Lamya was loquacious, but Basit too. Most of the time Basit would be in Lamya's room and would do his homework with her. The family had an air of love in their home. Children loved playing with their gadgets, but they had their traditional family culture, too. They would sit together in the evenings and play monopoly or hangman. I was impressed from the first day by the way they were close to each other. Not once they made me feel that I was a stranger. I was obliged to them heartily, for giving me the sense of what a family is, a family that I dreamt once to have, with Riz. I was no more taciturn, especially in presence of Lamya and Basit. They both were adorable and would not let me entomb myself for once. If they ever saw me quiet, they would start asking me the reason. Amna was a housewife, so she really needed a companion to talk to. She would often say that being a housewife is a tough and monotonous job with the least chances of escape. Still she was managing everything so well, that it seemed that it's the best job in the world.

I spoke to Amna that I really needed a job before my visit expired and she spoke to her husband, who gave me different websites and asked me to drop my CV. He also gave my CV in his office, but for two weeks there was no call for an interview. I started getting panicked, as I knew that there was no way back home. I had already resigned, and all my saving was spent on the air ticket and the visa. Saad suggested that I shouldn't try in schools only, as there were fewer chances to get the job of a teacher, during the school year. He told me as well that there was no such thing as a comfort zone and I might not get my desirable field. Amna observed that anxiousness had overtaken me and I was lost in my thoughts whenever I was alone. She advised me to think of changing my career, at least to get the visa and settle down. I started applying for all kinds of jobs which were of entry-level. One day I got an email from a water purification company for an interview. There was nothing mentioned regarding post or salary. The interview was to be in the morning, so I had to go by myself. Before leaving, Amna quietly slipped a note of two-hundred dirhams. I stared at her and had nothing to say. I couldn't say no, because I had no cash with me. I hugged her and started to cry. She tapped my back,

"Oh dear, don't worry, I will take a big treat once you get your first salary!"

I started to laugh with running nose.

Before I left, she instructed me like a concerned mother to recite verses from the Quran. I smiled and nodded. I went downstairs and I started looking for the cab. After standing ten minutes in the scorching sun, I saw the cab and started waving my hand. Once it stopped, I got in and showed him the address I had written on the paper.

"Okay, it's in Dubai. Near the Al Rigga Metro Station."

"Will it take time?"

"Depends on traffic." He replied.

"How much will it charge?"

"Depends on the meter. Are you new, here?"

I was confused and then noticed a device with the screen showing the charge. I had never seen such thing in Pakistan. Choosing a cab there always meant a lot of bargaining and picking the one that offered minimum rate.

"Yes. I have an interview."

"Are you alone, here?" By that time I had judged that the man was from my country, so if I had told him I had come to Dubai alone, he would have judged my character. I replied, "No, I live with my sister. My brother-in-law was at work, so I had to take cab."

He didn't say a word. A minute later he started asking me questions like when I came to Dubai, why I came and more, which made me uneasy, but I had no idea how to avoid. Once I reached my destination I was a bit disappointed to see the fare. It was too high, but I had to pay. I went inside the building and looked around for a lift. I went inside and saw so many buttons showing so many floors. I got out of the lift on the floor number which was written with me and started walking to left. The corridors were like a maze, never ending. Suddenly I saw a man coming out of an office. I stopped and asked politely,

"Can you please tell me where the Aqua Dream's office is?"

"What's the office number?"

"213."

"It will be near the lift."

I thanked him and started walking. Once I reached to the lift, I walked to the other side and discovered that office was right after two doors. I entered inside and found a Filipino lady sitting at a reception desk.

"Hi."

"Hello, Madame!" She greeted me in a friendly manner.

"I am here for an interview."

"What's your name?"

"Pari Sultan." I found my surname so strange and new. It sounded so alien to hear my surname from my own mouth.

"Please be seated, ma'am."

She asked me to follow her inside the office which was a glass room. I saw only one person, who was sitting. He introduced himself as Shaw. He extended his hand to shake mine. I thought for a moment and held the hand. It's against the Islamic faith to shake hand with the opposite gender. I was already sinful and any mistake I ever made would remind me of my old mistakes, mistakes where I stood against my faith for a mere human being.

Shaw was polite in his expressions and made me comfortable through appreciation, while looking at my resume. He turned to me and started, "Pari, you have an exceptionally great background in education and achievements. I'm afraid that you might not fit in this company, as we are new and the work is quite different from what you expect!"

I didn't know what to take that as, whether a rejection or a compliment. I cleared my throat, "I understand that I might not be fully aware of the field, but I am all ready to learn. I am here on a visit visa and I really need a work before it expires."

"But that would be a hard work."

"I am ready for that."My voice had persistency in it.

"I like your passion. I hope it stays till the end."

"It will."

"We will be paying you 2000AED only, as the company is new and not in a position to pay more."

I got the job and that was the only thing I was concerned about.

"No problem."

He looked at me thoughtfully, assuming how much in need of a job I was.

"Okay, bring your documents, so that we can send them to process the visa."

I gave him a full grin. He told me they didn't have much staff, yet, so he would be explaining me the complete duties after I would sign an offer letter. He thoroughly told that it was a small company which provided water purification system for household. My job would be to make calls to people and brief them about the product. I had to convince them to set an appointment to see a demonstration at their place. The rest of the things were to be explained after I would join. I went out of the building and quickly dialled Amna's number, "Amna!" I was so loud that a man passing by turned around.

"Mabrook!" She used the Arabic word for congratulating.

"How did you know that?" I was surprised.

"Your voice, dear. I am happy. Come fast, so we four can celebrate." She was referring to children, herself and me. Of course Saad wouldn't be coming before evening. I took the cab back to home and this time I had to call Amna to explain the directions to the driver. I had never been good at road mapping and there was no chance I would have remembered the address of Amna's place. Once I reached I paid the money and this time I asked him to keep the change. *I will pay back all the money to Amna as soon as I get the salary,* I thought in my heart. I quickly went to the apartment and rang the door. It seemed Amna was waiting for me. She gave me a big hug and started swinging me. She quickly set the table and waited for children. They would come by bus normally. Meanwhile I told her about the job and the manager. I told her how much they agreed to pay, and she said "But that's surely less."

"It's okay. I will manage. I just need to settle down first."

We didn't talk much about it and then we had lunch when children arrived.

In the evening, when Saad came back home, he asked the details of the company. He called his several friends to know if that was a good place to work or not. He was concerned for me as I really was their responsibility. He told me he would go with me to the office the next day.

At night, when Basit and Lamya were doing homework, Amna came and sat with me. I had made my routine to check their homework and books every day. I loved helping them in projects and assignments. Amna made the tea for me and herself and we sat down in the small room of Lamya.

"Lamya room is not big enough for even one and I Mom is having a high tea," Basit said looking at us.

"You go in your room and make some space here!" Amna teased him. Basit was taller than all of us but still a baby in his mind.

"Pari, do you know Mrs. Hisham?"

I thought for a moment, but I couldn't recall.

"She sometimes comes with her son who is Basit's classmate and taller than Basit. She lives in next building," she made it clearer.

I recalled her in a few seconds and said, "oh yes."

"Well, she came today and was asking if you could help her son in his studies. Basit told them you teach him and Lamya maths, so probably that's why she asks for tuitions."

"But I will be busy with my work from now on."

"But in evening you will be free, right?"

At that time I decided to tell Amna that I was hoping to move from her place after getting my first salary. I couldn't carry the guilt of burdening the family.

"After one month I would shift to some place near my office."

"Shift?" Lamya, who was apparently not at all listening, was the first one to show surprise.

"This is so unfair. So you never considered me as your sister," Amna turned gloomy.

"No, Amna, that's not the reason. That can never be the reason. You are the one who has taken care of me in my hardest times. I will always be indebted to you."

I expressed my feelings with the wrong words and this made Amna sadder.

"I never made you feel indebted."

"I know. But, you see, I can't bother you with my problems anymore and, trust me, I would have moved even if I was in my real sister's home."

"Okay, leave that topic for now. First you need to find a place and that would take time. Now tell me what I shall say to Mrs. Hisham." Amna had the quality of making every strained situation light.

"Well, what does she want me to teach her son?"

"Mathematics and sometimes he needs help in science projects too," Basit answered.

I looked at him and smiled, "Seems like you have a definite plan to trouble me with your friend."

"He is such a nice boy. Quiet and calm. I would exchange Basit for him, if his mother agreed," Lamya said, and we both giggled.

"Yeah, yeah. I'll ask her tomorrow to have me as her only beloved son," Basit teased his mom.

"Is he the only child?" I asked.

He nodded.

"What's his name?"

"Faiz," Basit said.

Twenty-three

After submitting my documents I was told to join them since Saturday, which is the first working day in Dubai for most private companies. After joining, Shaw explained me how things worked in the company. The company had two representatives, at that moment, who would come and explain how the machine actually worked. The company was collecting data in two processes; first, Shaw had a friend in a bank who provided him with the list of the account holders, with their complete details, including their salary. I was surprised on this fact and Shaw, reading my face, immediately advised me not to share the information with anyone and if a customer asked how we got the number, then I should reply "through a company's representative". Second, during daytime representatives even the receptionist would go to addresses from that list and carry out the process which in company's terminology was called 'door-knocking'. Reps would greet people with a warm and friendly smile and would recite the script written by Shaw.

Good Morning, Ma'am/Sir. I am a representative from Aqua Dream Water Purification. We are distributing raffle coupons for our water purification system. The draw will be at the end of our month, there is no fee or charge, but you just have to give your name and phone number. Our telemarketer will call you from the head office.

Residents would be happy to find out that they were getting a free coupon and no doubt they never wanted to miss a chance, if they could get something free. After the appointment got confirmed the representative would go to the customer's place and show them a magic demonstration. He would ask them to bring three glasses: one glass filled with tap water, one with mineral water and in the last he would pour the bottle purified through the Aqua Dreams Purification System. Then the representative would put electrode rods in the water and let the show begin. The water in the first glass would turn black, the second would change to dark brown and the last one would not change more than to pale yellow. Then the clients would be explained how dangerous the tap and the mineral water could be for their health. Those highly concerned would immediately make a payment; some asked for a day or two and after consulting their friends or a research on internet would change their mind. The sales representatives got ten percent profit on each sale, so if I made fewer appointments they would blame me.

The next task of my job was harder than I expected. It was called 'door-knocking'. In those buildings where the security was strict and our male representatives wouldn't get the permission to enter, I had to perform their task. I would pretend to be a visitor and move around the corridors, ringing the bell of every door. Some ladies would look at me sympathetically, other would just cast a disgusting look and some would be indifferent. For most of the traditional housewives, a working woman is a sign of boldness and of a weaker character. There definitely were men who looked at me as an object which could be attracted, flirted with and left. But to my surprise most of the men would greet me with respect, and they would listen to me patiently. They never shut the door on my face. Women, on the other side, never missed that chance. I assume they had a kind of fear of a robbery or theft. But Dubai was the place where I found myself most secured and protected. Even at night, I had no fear of walking alone on the streets. But, like every place, it has its own colours. There are women who work at night. These are women who earn their living during night. Whether a woman shows off her body or hides it completely, there are always people who judge her.

One day, I got into a building which had dark corridors. It was quiet and there was no one to be seen. Usually people would step back quietly when they would see me from the door hole. They could easily assume that I was there to promote some product and would let me wait for ten minutes and, eventually, after a long wait, I'd leave. Sometimes I wished I could tell them to just tell me once to leave the door. I wished I could give them the confidence that one straight refusal would not break my heart, like a long wait filled with hope actually did. I wanted to tell them not to feel vulnerable as they were safe inside their houses. But their conscious or ego would never let them say no. That day, I rang several doors and nobody opened. I could see the light in door hole getting dark when someone would look out and then there would be a never ending silence. I reached to the end of the corridor then decided to move back. I started walking to the lift from where I entered, when suddenly the last door which I rang was opened. Three boys emerged in shorts and pants. They started following me and asking how much I would charge. My legs started shaking and my heart was pounding. I started to run, but one of them blocked my way. Although they seemed drunk, they still made sure not to speak loudly. Suddenly, the first door opened and a lady came out. She didn't see me and started to put the key in the key hole to lock the door. She was in saree and with the bag in her hand. It was obvious that she was leaving for somewhere. Seeing my own gender gave me confidence and I spoke loudly, *"Get away!"* She heard my voice and turned around and all the three boys ran into their apartment. She stopped there and waited for me; I walked to her, assuming that she cared. She looked at me from head to toe, "From your dress, you don't look like one. What made you sleep with them?"

"What?" I couldn't grasp what she said.

"Ladies like you have no shame, and no respect for us that we live here with families and children. You only need money!"

She reached to the lift, and, once the door opened, she turned to me, "Let me go alone. I don't want people to see me coming out with some whore!"

"Whore? You are wrong!"

She shrugged, pressed the lift button and left.

I took another elevator and left the building. I came out and sat by the road on the hot, burning brick and cried. I could be everything but not a whore. *How could she judge me? I can't do this door-knocking work.* But I had no other option.

After collecting data, I would go back to office to submit it and then go home. Shaw wasn't happy with my progress. There was no direct sale by me. He wanted me to perform exceptionally well in tasks of telemarketing and door-knocking. By the time I would reach Sharjah, it would be nine in the evening. There would always be a long queue of cars going from Dubai to Sharjah. Most people worked in Dubai, but lived in Sharjah due to the cost of living. Meanwhile, I started to search a place where I could move and manage to do it within 2000 AED. When I started hunting the place, I discovered how expensive the accommodation was. There was nothing as such like 1000 AED for a studio room. The only cheapest option which was available was to share a room. It was a hard decision, but I had to avail that. I kept looking for a room for sharing in classified newspaper and websites.

One day, when I reached home, I found Basit sitting in the lounge and playing PlayStation with his friend Faiz. I entered in the room and they both stood in respect. Faiz was surely taller and shier than Basit.

"Pari *Khala*, he is Faiz," Basit introduced him to me.

"Hi, Faiz. I am Pari. Basit's aunt."

"Yeah, he told me," he said. Even though he spoke, he still appeared quiet.

I went inside the room to change, then came out and sat with the boys.

"So Faiz, what do you do?"

"I study."

"And what do you do, in your free time?"

"Football," he specified.

"Do you watch or play football?"

"Both."

"Basit told me you need some help in studies. "

"Yeah."Another short answer.

"What subjects, dear?" I intently called him dear so he could relax.

"Maths and Physics."

I turned to Basit, "Does your friend always speak little, or is it the first time?"

"He is abnormal, in school," and he started laughing. Faiz stared at him and smiled and didn't comment. *It might because he is meeting me for the first time that's why he is shy.* I thought to myself.

Amna appeared from the kitchen and asked everyone to wash their hands. She spread the sheet on the carpet and I started helping her in putting the dishes. There was a dining table in the corner of the living room but with four chairs. It was occasionally used, but regular meals were always taken in the traditional way. During dinner I noticed Faiz ate rice with the hands. He didn't put much food in his plate, rather too little for a boy of his age. After dinner I thought to set the timings for Faiz. I told him I would help him on Thursday evenings and on Friday mornings for two hours. After work it was too hectic, for me, to take any class. On Thursdays I was allowed to leave early, as the traffic would be blocked some time for two to three hours on weekend. Amna came out of the kitchen and informed Faiz that his mom was calling him back home. He took his phone from his pocket and I guess he noticed the missed calls from his mom. He seemed worried and left immediately.

After my first salary, I found a room on sharing near Amna's apartment. I tried my best to get something near my place, but the accommodation was unaffordable, there. I shifted into three bedrooms in the apartment and in each room there were four girls. There were two bathrooms, both on sharing, and a kitchen which had to be used by everyone. I was quite used to this, as in the hostel there were almost eighty girls and only nine toilets. There were four sinks outside in the open air to wash face and hands. I was sure adjusting wouldn't be a problem. When I told Amna, initially she wasn't happy, but she agreed. She herself knew that I couldn't stay in her house forever. She provided me with home essentials and some dishes. The rest, I managed with my salary. After paying rent, travelling and food expense, I would only be left with 500 each month. After spending some I would save the rest.

Faiz started coming to my new place on Thursdays and Fridays. Slowly he started getting friendlier. He was eighteen years old and almost eight years younger than me. I started looking at him like a baby brother whom I always wished to have, but I avoided any kind of expression. Slowly, Faiz started getting attached to me and he would share everything with me. He told me how he wished to have a sister and how he found one in me. I would smile at his childish expressions. Basit told me that Faiz had become a very calm person at school.

"*Khala*, do you know that Faiz doesn't fight with anyone, at school, now?" One day when I was at their home Basit broke this news.

I smiled, "Did he use to fight?"

"A lot. All the time."

"Why so?"

"I don't know," he shrugged. "He loses his cool on every little thing."

Amna, who was watching television, was also hearing our conversation.

"I guess, Pari, he has some family problems," she said.

"But he is an only child," after the words slipped out of my mouth I realized it was a foolish excuse.

"Yes. But being an only child doesn't guarantee the love of your parents." I agreed. My heart melted for that boy with deep black eyes. He had lot of passion and sadness in them. I started giving him more of my time, though he would not get the permission from his parents to hang out with his friends or to go out without any reasonable excuse. He started chatting with me every day and his messages were long and detailed. He would send me paragraphs on his day. What did he do in the morning, how were the classes, what he had for lunch and all the minor details. I didn't find those things peculiar; rather, I started getting kinder and caring, with him. I understood the loneliness he was going through and that was common for an only child. After work I would often go to Amna's place and stayed there for an hour or two. She started noticing my utmost attention on the phone and one day she started teasing me, "All day I wait for you so that you come and I talk my stuff with you, but now you are always occupied with this mini-machine!"

I knew where she was heading, so I kept the phone aside, but my eyes were constantly on the screen hoping that my delay in replying mightn't hurt Faiz.

"Tell me, I'm all here for you."

"No. You are there where the sender of those messages is."

I couldn't hide my laughter and I took her in my arms.

"You are terribly mistaken!" I laughed.

"Tell me who is there, then?" She winked and I knew it was time to tell her before she might start assuming things wrong.

"Oh, wait. Wait. He is no other but Faiz." I held the phone in my hand and turned the screen towards her. I opened his messages and saw in a minute he left several messages,

"Where are you Baaji, sister?*"* Amna read loudly.

I smiled, "See, that's what I told you. He starts getting panic if I don't reply him back."

"Baaji?" She laughed.

"Yeah, he asked me if it's okay to call me *Baaji.* I said whatever he likes."

"Oh, *Baaji* or teacher, whatever. I had butterflies in stomach."

"For what?"

"Well, I thought there is someone special."

"Oh, dear! He is special too. He is my baby brother," I grinned.

"You know well what I mean by 'special'." She couldn't be more vivid in her expression.

Twenty-four

Days passed by and I got busier and busier with my job. I would hardly get any time for myself. On the weekend, which was only on Friday, I just wanted to sleep. I was glad that exhaustion overtook my moroseness and I stopped blaming fate for all the bad events occurred to me. Things were going smoothly, Faiz was busy with his annual exams and I would just see him on the weekends. I would go to Amna's place after work and after coming back would directly sleep. She would never let me go without dinner. From time to time I would call Furqan and my professor. I realized that I might not have had a normal family with blood ties, but whoever so far had stayed with me during trials were all I had. They were my only family and I never wanted to lose them. In my physical world I was confined to Amna, her children and Faiz. I accepted Faiz not only as a brother but my own child. Often Amna would slightly reprimand me for getting so much attached to him.

"Pari, think about yourself. One day this boy will leave."

"To where?" I would ask carelessly.

"He has no relation with you. No blood ties. He isn't your brother. And your own brothers left you." By the end of a year I had shared with her everything, except Rizwan.

"That's the difference. Those were step brothers. Faiz is mine! My very own!"

"But not your real brother," she was persistent.

"You aren't my real sister, but you are more than Salma and Sobia. They never called me once and here you took me into your house and sheltered me. Because I have no blood ties with you. Blood isn't important."

She shrugged her shoulders, "It's hard to make you understand."

Faiz won't go. He won't change because he needs me. I needed Rizwan, but he didn't need me, so he left. I won't leave and neither Faiz will! My heart would say. I started believing only the people who stay are the ones who need us. More than adoring Faiz I wanted to keep him happy. I wanted to give love to anyone who was in need of it. I stopped seeking the shade of a tree; rather I started looking for people who were burning in the sunlight. I started taking the mission of a cloud, and in that process I was healing my own soul. I started to heal, since it was love which was healing me again. Love with no physical desire but rather purity. Love without the connection of bodies but rather souls. I had no idea why I loved Faiz so much that, whatever money I would have, I'd spend it in buying little presents for him. I couldn't go to sleep without talking to him and would not leave for work without getting his good morning text. He became my friend, my brother and my son.

Faiz had lost several friends due to his house rules. He would never get permission from his mother to hang out so slowly he started losing friends. He was no doubt an extraordinary student, but he was so poor at expressing love that he also lost his girlfriend whom he considered his greatest joy. I saw my reflection in him; I would tell him my past events to explain to him that he was not the only one to go through such things and strictness. When I started narrating him the events he would often be so surprised that our lives in both childhood and teenage years were so similar. He started calling me "half soul". I believed him because I thought he was a child and children don't lie when it comes to heart. He became friendly and warm. My past started to fade and I kept myself busy in shading him with my love. He would read my mind and force me to share my problems with him. He would guess with certainty if I hid something in my heart and forced me to tell him. He wanted me to consider him as my best friend. One day, when we were in the library and I was helping him in preparing his university entrance exam, he asked to take some break.

"Go drink some water. We will start in ten minutes. I know you are tired."

"I am okay."

"What happened?" I read his face.

"Nothing."

"Tell me, Faiz *bachay*, my child."

"I will tell you. You know that."

"I know," I smiled.

"But you are still hiding something."

"What?" I loved his stubbornness.

"You know that. Your eyes say all."

"My eyes?" I laughed and a man two desks away stared at us.

"See, people are looking at us. Don't make noise."

"I know you will never tell me."

"My God! I will. Give me some time."

"Why?" He asked.

I couldn't say I needed time to trust him, it would probably hurt him.

"Faiz, when I share my secrets with someone I can't let that person go. I have not ever shared this specific thing with anyone."

"So you don't trust me. Well..."

"Here you are again. I never meant to say that!"

"I am not going anywhere. You know. Where will I go? *Baaji*, you are my sister!"

I trusted him. I told him everything about Riz. I started telling the events one by one and it ended on a sad note. Once I finished I looked at him on a hope to hear something, but he didn't. He got the call from his mom and he said he needed to go home.

"All right, I will go home too. It's quiet late. "

While we were walking home, I turned to him, "Faiz, what do you think of what I told?"

"Nothing. What was his caste?" His question startled me. That was the least thing I expected him to say. I had no answer and I opened my mouth to say something, but he cut in, "Let me guess. Hmm...Punjabi?" He grinned.

What is there to smile about? I shouldn't have told him. I wanted it to be untold.

I reached home and bade him good bye. I was disappointed and wondered why he never said something else. Faiz observed that I was ignoring him and he asked the reason, which I told him and he got upset.

"I never meant that. Do you know how upset I was to hear that my sister has been through so much pain?"

"I'm sorry. I just thought you are too young to understand these emotions."

"I probably am young, but I do understand your feelings."

I was sorry for I shouldn't have doubted him. We would fight like siblings and I never took those fights seriously, but I was concerned not to hurt him. He was difficult to understand and it was probably because he was a teenager. I never had any experience with teenagers, so in my free times I would borrow books from library and read about the mood changes in teens. I wanted to be the best sister in the world after failing so many relations. I started celebrating little and big events with him, from his birthday to getting passed in an exam. He became the centre of my universe and I kept myself occupied with his happiness. I would always rush back home fast because he would not sleep without my good night message. It gave me a happiness that I always sought, a feeling of being needed. I never minded if I had to stay up long to chat with him during his vacation and get up early. Disappointing him was the last thing I considered.

But after a few months, things started changing. He started talking less and would make excuses of being busy and occupied with exams. I insisted if there was something he could share with me, but he would always reply, "*Baaji*, you know I share everything with you. I'm just busy."

My instincts told me that things were changing, but I decided not to believe them.

Twenty-five

During all this I was also occupied with lot of work in my office. My job was draining the energy out of me and the salary was also not issued on time. On my offer letter I was promised I would be paid on 5th of every month, but sometimes it would be issued on 17th. I sometimes regretted joining the company, as there was no progress and almost no sales.

Our CEO Ram Das was an uneducated businessman who actually ran the grocery, but someone gave him the idea about water purification. He was persistent that people in Dubai really care for their health, as they are buying the water for drinking, unlike third world countries where people hardly have access to clean water. If he would ever see me and Janet sitting free in the office he would ask Shaw why he didn't provide us with data to call on, so we always had to be active and busy.

Then, one day, one of the sale representatives quit the job, so Shaw had to hire someone again. This time he didn't conduct the interviews, but hired someone through his reference. The new employee was Jabir and he was working in an established company in the same field. He was known to make lots of sales and had a great command in marketing. Shaw wanted someone who was already skilled in the field and could train the rest of the staff. He offered him a higher package than his previous company and tried his best to compel him.

Finally, Jabir joined the company and he started making new rules. He was thin, had long hair and cleaned shaved. His stare had something which would always make me uncomfortable. He never appreciated if anyone would say no to him. He didn't like taking orders from Shaw or even Ram. The company needed profit at any cost and they were obliged to follow whatever he asked. No doubt he was good at sales and within the first week he gave the company a big profit by selling the machine to a labour camp. He sold the giant system with the capacity to purify 800 gallons of water in a day. Definitely the company made its first high profit through this sale as they got many more contacts from the owner of the company.

No matter how open and warming I had become at Amna's place, in the professional world it was hard for me to break the shell. My only communication was with Shaw as he was the one taking care of my data. After Jabir joined I never changed my routine of submitting reports to Shaw. This didn't make Jabir happy and he never missed an opportunity to criticize me and my work.

Jabir started taking the sales representatives with him on demonstrations and insisted that I should go with him too. I told Shaw that I wouldn't accompany him at any cost, but he suggested that I should go for once, and later he would make an excuse for me. The appointment was fixed on Thursday and it was at 4:00 PM. Shaw told me that after the meeting with the customer I could go home. I was dithery, but had no other choice than to go with Jabir. My instincts were telling me to make some excuse and escape from the meeting, but I couldn't find the courage to do so. Jabir drove the car and after reaching to the customer's house he called him before going. He dialled his number and after talking to him for few minutes he turned to me and said, "He cancelled the appointment."

"Oh. Okay I'll go home then. I'll inform Shaw."

"I'll drop you."

I wasn't comfortable with that at all. I turned to him and firmly said, "I can go by myself."

"Why are you so stubborn and rude? What have I done to you?"

"I'm not stubborn and rude; I just said I can go by myself."

Without saying anything he started the car.

"Don't you understand?" I was harsh.

"Your Mr. Shaw told me to drop you at your place."

The way he used "Your" made me furious, "Mind your words!"

He didn't say anything. He kept driving and I was thinking in my head how to get rid of him. I didn't want to show him my anger. I held my phone in hand and thought to message Shaw that call and ask Jabir to drop me at office. Suddenly he said, "On my way I have to pick something from my sister's place."

I was glad that I could leave the car and was surprised as I had never heard of his sister. He was living on sharing and had no family there. I decided to stay quiet and not to comment. After ten minutes we were in the colony International City. It's a residential area with communities themed as Spain, China and other countries. Though there are lot of people who live there, as accommodation is cheaper than other parts of Dubai, but it has a quiet environment. People from all culture live there and due to busy life they do not get much time to communicate with neighbours. I had visited that place once with Janet and we went there by bus as there is no access by metro to that area. Janet had been in Dubai for seven years and was well acquainted with all the areas. Jabir asked me to wait in the car and I was disappointed that I could not leave his car, as there was no bus stop nearby and I couldn't afford the luxury of a cab. I decided to call Shaw and work on the first thought of going to the office. As soon as I held the phone it started ringing and the screen showed *Jabir calling. What is it now?*, I thought. I answered the call, "Yeah?" I asked without any hello.

"I have forgotten a bag in the car. It's on the back seat. Could you please bring it upstairs?"

"What? Why?" I was not sure what to reply.

"I need it. It has some presents for my nephew which I need to give. Please can you hurry so we can go back early?"

I tried to process all he said in my mind and was not sure how to say no.

"Are you there?"

"Which floor?" I broke my silence.

"3rd floor. 302."

I put down the phone. *Why is he telling me the flat number? I'm not stepping out of the lift.* I thought angrily.

I took the bag and went inside the building and let the car engine run. Inside the lift, before pressing the button, I opened the bag and saw there were some toys unwrapped. When I came out of the lift I couldn't see him anywhere. I called him again, "Come to the lift and take the bag," I announced without waiting for him to say anything.

"Oh. I'm having a tea. Just come to the door. It's near," and he spoke to someone at the back, "Zainab go and open the door, my colleague is waiting outside," then he spoke to me again, "Zainab is at the door," and he hung up. I walked to 302 unwillingly and found the door ajar. I rang the bell and heard the sound of a television in the background. I knocked and moved my hand inside the door to push it slightly. Before I could peep inside someone grabbed my hand and pulled me inside and shut the door at my back.

Twenty-six

Jabir put his hand on my mouth tightly and dragged me in the lounge. I couldn't scream but kept fighting with my arms. He bent my arm tightly and after a while I started getting exhausted.

"Not today!" He laughed.

I couldn't open my mouth. He pushed me onto the sofa and placed his mouth in my neck. He was a beast whom I couldn't fight. As I started to lose energy while fighting him back I closed my eyes tightly and prayed silently. I needed a miracle and he was making sure that it wouldn't be happening. He moved back and loosened the grip of his hand on my mouth. I recollected all the energy I could and pushed his hand back and shouted all I could think of, "Allah! Help!"

He got panicked and slapped me hard on my face. "One more word and I'll kill you here."

"Please leave me," I begged with tears.

"Give me what I want and then you are free to go."

"For Allah's sake leave me! Have little faith in your heart!"

He laughed like a monster, "Haven't you given this to Shaw? Give me too, at least unlike him I'm from your own religion."

He took my light conversations with Shaw in entirely wrong way. What was he assuming all that time? *I won't die without fighting!* I thought and tried to free myself. He was neither tall nor bulky; he always looked underweight. I was surprised to find an apparently thin-looking man could have so much power. Seeing me not giving up he grabbed the cushion and put it on my mouth. He was threatening me or really wanted to kill me, I couldn't understand.

After doing it long enough to make me believe that he would really suffocate me, he removed the cushion and took a knife from his pocket and forced me to stop struggling. He removed my head cover and untied my hair. He took out his phone, "If you won't shut up, I'll post this video on YouTube."

"You will suffer!"

He pushed me down, "Just shut up!"

He started acting like a maniac. He started to smoke. After finishing three cigarettes he brought a drink and a glass from kitchen. He was back in less than a minute. It seemed he had been planning that for long. I had no idea what the time was, for me it had stopped already.

Suddenly what happened was something I would have never expected. There was a bang on the front door. He threw the cigarette and ran towards the door. I screamed again, "Help!"

He looked out from the spy hole and then looked back at me. He was in utter shock. His lips were dried and he started looking around and then looked at the window. He moved towards it and moved the curtain. The window had probably been locked for long time and he couldn't open it at once. I ran towards the door, but there was no key in the key hole. I started beating the door and suddenly I heard a man's voice, "Get aside, sister, I will break the door." I moved aside and covered my head with the scarf.

My shirt was torn from the shoulder and I tried to hide it with the scarf and my hand. After a few minutes, with a loud sound the door fell down. Jabir couldn't open the window and he turned pale to see four male and one female police officers. They pointed the gun towards Jabir and ordered him to kneel down. One ran towards him and pushed him on the floor and put handcuffs on his wrists. They arrested him and took him out of the room.

I was shivering with fear and couldn't walk out. The officers told me to relax and told that a boy from the grocery shop came to deliver some stuff on the same floor. He heard some noise and informed the watchman, who watched the recording of the CCTV camera and saw someone pushing me inside. He immediately called the police and it took them less than ten minutes to reach. They assured me that I would be given justice and protection and I just needed to file the case against the culprit. They continued calling me 'sister' and not at once spoke to me loudly. They asked me to call my family and tell them to go to police station directly.

"I have no family but a cousin. I will call her."I told them a half truth.

"It's okay. Call her. Will she come?"

"Yes. She is like a sister to me."

"Okay. Call her, then."

I dialled Amna's number and after a few minutes she answered. As soon as I heard her voice I started crying.

"Pari! My girl! What's wrong?"

And with sniffles I told her all that happened.

"What? My God! Where are you now?"

"They are taking me to the police station. Can you come?"

She evasively asked, "Which police station?"

I turned to the lady officer and asked her where they should come. She told me the address. I explained to Amna and she said she would call Saad. After finishing the call I went downstairs and I noticed how people hanging on their doors immediately went inside when they saw the police. I hid my face and started wondering what gossips now they would circulate. *I have lost all my dignity today.* I thought. I went downstairs and saw one patrol car and Jabir wasn't inside. They had already taken him.

We reached the police station and the police filed my report and gave me the confidence that the man couldn't at any chance get a release. One of the senior officers explained me kindly about the judiciary system of UAE. He told me that women rights are higher in UAE than in any part of the world. After my report they sent me for a medical examination and once it was finished I was told to go home and that they would call. I was surprised that even after two hours Saad or Amna didn't come. I called them worriedly, but no one answered. I left the police station and went out on the road. Once again, I was alone. I was back to the time when I left Riz's flat. That night Amir found me. *I wish I had never come to Dubai. I should have accepted Amir.* I burst into tears in the air-conditioned room of a bus stop. Luckily there was no one there and I cried my heart out. I left a message to Amna, "I have left the police station. I'm coming home." There was no reply for the next ten minutes. I called on Basit's phone and he answered immediately,

"Pari Aunty, come fast, mom has made meat balls." He sounded cheerful and unaware of the recent event. But as soon as he said that, I heard the whispers on the call.

"Where is mom?"

"Mm..Mom? Yeah. One minute," he put the phone on hold and after almost two minutes of silence he came on phone, "Pari Aunty, she is not at home. She has gone with Dad at some friend's house."

My mind couldn't grasp this and I tried to comprehend whatever he said. I made an explanation in my head; *Probably she was already there when I called her. That's why she couldn't come.*

"Basit, when did she leave?"

"Hmm, ten minutes ago." His voice was weak.

I understood that Basit was forced to lie. Amna didn't want to talk to me. She and her husband did not want to get involved into anything that had something to do with the police. I felt cold in the conditioned air and went out on the road and hot breeze touched my face. I got on the bus and I kept wondering what more I had to lose.

I couldn't sleep all night. I kept tossing and turning with the flashbacks of the past. I knew the next thing was to decide what I should do next. *Shall I go back?* It was a hard decision and there was no way back home. My brain started wandering and I started thinking of committing a suicide. I thought of the options available, but none seemed to work. I realized what a coward I was, although all my life I was told that to kill oneself is an act of a coward.

Next morning at 8:00 o'clock I got a call from the police station and they asked me to go there. Before leaving I called Amna, but she didn't answer. I couldn't blame her. She already had done enough for me and now that was my own battle. Life is actually our own battle and the less we depend on the others to fight with us, the happier we are. I reached the police station and they told me that my case had been sent to the court. They assured me that my case would not take more than two hearings, as there were a witness and the camera recording.

While I was there, Shaw came. He was also called to the police station and was asked about the appointment. They asked Shaw to call the client and ask him about the reason for cancelling the meeting. He made the call in front of the officers, "Hello, Mr. Rajesh. I'm Shaw from Aqua Dream Water Purification. I'm calling for a quality check. May I know if the appointment made with you yesterday was cancelled by you or our representative?"

"Hi, no, a guy called me in the morning and I cancelled it the same time." We heard him through speakers.

"Can you tell the name of the person who called you?" Shaw asked.

"Ah.. I guess Jasim.. no something started with J," he stressed on his memory, "I think Jabir. Yeah, right. Jabir."

"Did he call you in the afternoon?"

"No, he didn't. What happened?"

"Nothing, Sir. We are just doing a survey," he thanked the client and hung up.

Police asked Shaw to keep things confidential. After he left, the police asked me to appear in the court two days later. I went back to my room and called Shaw, "I can't work there anymore. If you could ask the boss to fire me, you'd spare me from resigning. As you know if I resign I'll get a six months ban and I wouldn't get another job easily." He assured me he would cooperate as much as possible. He said he was sorry.

My roommate asked me why I wasn't going to work and I said I lost a job. Days went by and neither Amna nor Faiz called me. I was surprised by how they could keep on living without me. I really wanted to know if they cared, or missed me.

Sometimes I would imagine myself on my death bed where the call of my illness would make them rush to see me. In those thoughts I wondered if Riz would come too. My past started living again. My demons never died. They only were asleep for some time and now they were back.

After two days I went to the court and I was sent to the ladies section. There was a judge, a lawyer, two police officers and Jabir. The trial didn't take long as Jabir admitted he was guilty. He said he just wanted to scare me because I was rude to him at work. The judge sentenced him with two years of jail and imposed the fine. I came out of the court and marvelled at how simply I got the justice. Without any embarrassing questions and delay in trials my case was solved in a single hearing.

I looked up at the sky and asked silently, *What's next?* I started walking along the road and wondered where was Faiz. I sat down in a café and called him. He didn't answer. I went on Facebook and I saw his photo with a cute girl posted a few days ago with the caption, *With the love of my life.* My eyes were wet. I wasn't jealous. I wasn't envious. I was happy for my little boy, but why didn't he tell me? Why he never broke this new to me? I went through the girl's page and discovered he had been in a relationship with her for months. He never told me. Whenever he wouldn't reply I asked him the reason and he said he was busy. He made excuses that his mom didn't let him use the phone. I was shocked to read his conversation under one of the photos, where he posted, "I don't have to appreciate anyone else in my life, just you."

So my chapter was over in his life. I never ended the relations in my life and I couldn't do that with Faiz too. I called him several times, but he didn't answer. He finally called back when I reached home.

"Hi." His voice was awkward.

"Where were you?" *Has Basit said something to him?* I wondered.

"Exams," he replied.

"Why are you talking like this?"

"Like what?"

"Nothing. Tell me, how are you and how are things going?"

"Busy as usual."

"You were never too busy to reply me."

"Why are you now making an issue?" His tone changed.

"Faiz? I'm not making an issue. Just asking."

"I told you, nothing special."

"So how's your girlfriend?"

"What girlfriend?"

"I saw on Facebook."

"So now you know."

"Why did you hide it?"

"Hello? I didn't hide it! Stop blaming me!" He shouted.

I heard him shouting at me for first time.

"Don't misbehave!"

"You, don't make me misbehave!"

I was speechless. I closed my eyes and let the tears roll. I managed to speak, "You never asked what happened these seven days. You were busy with building new relations."

"I wasn't busy with her! I told you!"

He didn't ask what went wrong and I put down the phone. I was broken. I realised that he needed his space. He wanted me to stay away. His needs were over. His loneliness was filled. I was such a misfit in men's world. I couldn't beg Faiz to stay, but that day I realised I was attached to him more than he was. Amna was right, that there was such a time to come. A wrong time or right time, but whatever it was, it taught me a thousand years of learning during twenty-six years of my life. I learnt the lessons which no school and no curriculum could have ever taught me. I learnt the lessons which were painful and long lasting. The lessons which left marks and wisdom.

We human beings are the most abstract art of God. We have a tendency to mould imperfection into perfection. But we also have the weakness of not understanding the mystery lying behind the hearts that once showed us love. That was the lesson I carried with me before leaving Dubai. The city of colours and world records. The place with skyscrapers, peace, diversity and unity. A place where I grew confidence and where I lost one of the most precious relations. A boy whom I never gave birth, a brother who wasn't born from my mother's womb. A best friend who knew the darkest corners of my life. I gave him everything, love, care and happiness, but I couldn't give him trust. He was too young to trust me. I knew he was too stubborn to make me stay so I didn't tell him. I quietly left Dubai.

Twenty-seven

I reached Pakistan and I had no idea where to go. I took a cab and I went to the private hostel. I didn't have much money to spend on any hotel and no intention to risk my safety. I reached there and the hostel warden greeted me warmly. She was excited to see me back from abroad. I regretted not bringing any present for her. She immediately gave me a room and told me that due to summer vacations most of the rooms were empty. I was glad to have a room in solace.

The day after, I went out for a walk. I went to *Sadar*, a big market place in Rawalpindi to buy some stuff. I was in the mart when I saw Tania and her figure showed she was expecting. I smiled, but I didn't have any courage to socialize with the world. She saw me and shouted without bothering about the crowd, "Pari!" I smiled and reached her. She hugged me before I could open my arms.

"Tania! Congratulations!" I smiled.

She blushed, "It's my sixth month."

"I never knew you got married. I have been busy with job after university."

"Yes, I came to know you were in Dubai. You never posted any update on any social media."

"Because I am not social," I laughed.

"As if I don't know! You always had more friends in university than most of us."

I smiled. "Let's sit somewhere. Are you here with your husband?"

"Yeah. He dropped me off and has gone to finish some work. He'll be here in an hour."

"Okay let's go to the coffee shop."

We started walking towards the coffee shop. Tania ordered a coffee for me only.

"Won't you have something?" I asked.

"I avoid caffeine or intake of any junk."

I smiled and admired her for being such a caring mother. I got lost in my thoughts. *Faiz.* My heart sighed.

"I'll call my husband and give him a surprise."

"Surprise?" I smiled and frowned.

She signalled me to stay quiet as she had already dialled the number and put the mobile on her ear.

"Hey! I have a surprise for you. I found a lost friend of ours!" She announced to the person on the other side, "Well, I won't tell you the name. Come and see by yourself," she laughed, "No, we are not shopping. We are in the coffee bar. Okay. See you." She hung up the call and looked at me with a grin.

"What's going on?" I asked, puzzled.

"A surprise. You will see who I'm married to!"

I started recalling all the faces of the boys who were in our batch. I couldn't think of anyone whom Tina liked.

"I have no clue," I gave up.

"Only because you never stayed in touch. You escaped from all of us."

"There were reasons," I smiled.

She placed her hand on the back of my hand and said softly, "I know."

"You know? You know about my breakup?"

"Yeah. I know what he did to you. Trust me, he is not happy,"

I cut in on her, "Please, Tina. I don't want to know about him. Whether he is happy or miserable, it doesn't matter to me, now. He is not even a past, now. He is beyond that."

"I'm sorry." She meant it.

"It's okay. Tell me, where is your prince charming?" I teased her.

"Wait. Wait. He will be here."

"How's Hira?" I suddenly thought of her.

"She has gone to the US for doctorate."

I laughed, she never wanted to study after graduation, and now look at her!

"Yeah. Whenever I Skype with her I call her a traitor." We laughed.

"True. I wish I would have tried for a scholarship."

"At least you're better than me. You are working; I just got married and became a housewife."

"Home-maker! Don't underestimate your super powers!" I teased her.

Our conversation shifted to the university days and we recalled all the absurd things we did.

"What a puerile I was!" I laughed like a drain.

"Oh, don't say that! Those were golden days."

I felt my jaws were hurting and I was obliged to Tina for making me laugh.

"Where is your gentleman? I will die with curiosity!"

She picked up her phone to make a call, "Hey, where-" She was interrupted, "Ah! okay." She smiled and turned to me, "He is here, just parking the car."

"I can't wait!" I laughed. I started looking towards the door which was visible to me, but Tina's back was towards it. A minute later I saw him entering inside. He was walking towards us. He stared open-mouthed at me and then started to smile. My heart sank and I didn't know why. I said without a smile, "Amir?"

Twenty-eight

Tina cast an eye over me bemusedly and turned around, "Amir? What are you doing here?"

I was boggled and didn't know what to say, then I saw Musa walking in. He reached us and turned to me,

"Hey, Pari! What a surprise!"

"Isn't it a surprise? And where did you find Amir?" she turned to Musa.

At that moment I understood that Tina was married to Musa, not to Amir, and I felt a kind of relief and I tried to push my thoughts back.

"We were together, actually. He had some work so he asked me to stay."

"Or probably telepathy," Tina winked at Amir. He couldn't hide his smile.

"How are you, Pari?" Amir asked me.

"I'm good," I said.

I told them I came just a day before and I was staying in a hostel. Tina insisted that I should stay at her place, but I politely said that I would visit her someday. Tina was exhausted for sitting so long so I told them to go home and I promised I would visit them soon. Musa asked Amir to drop me back home and I couldn't say no. Once Tina and Musa left I turned to Amir, he sat down and asked me to sit.

"I will drop you. First tell me, for how long you are here?"

"I don't know. Maybe I'll go to Canada. Furqan has got a job. He is happy there. I am planning to get the documents ready and send them to him."

"Why? Aren't you going back to Dubai?"

"No. I lost that job. I miss Furqan. He is all I have, now."

"Now? Who else was there before? I mean…" he regretted asking the question.

"I understand. Some people I got close to in Dubai and made me think I was blessed with a family." I gave a fake smile.

"Who?" He asked seriously.

"Don't worry, I never had a boyfriend," I answered reading his expressions.

"I didn't mean that," he got embarrassed.

"Well, I had a friend who took care of me like a sister and I had a brother who was like a baby to me. I lost them both."

"Why?"

"Some unexpected and unacceptable events occurred in my life, so the former left me and for the later- I thought for a moment- maybe he is too young to understand how elders love or to *appreciate* each relation in his life." I intentionally used the word *appreciate* hoping that Faiz could hear me. *I wish telepathy worked…* I thought.

"I don't know what you have been through, but I admire you from the very first day. You are such a strong and dedicated person I have met. As I said two years ago, and I say it again, I need you, Pari. I want to keep you happy. I really love you." He was as in a trance.

I thought for a moment not to believe any single word of him and I gathered the words, "Then let me tell you what I have been through."

"I love you despite everything you may have been going through," he said immediately.

"You will stop. Eventually," I replied.

"I won't!"

"I was molested by my colleague. A man actually tried to..." I had tears in my eyes. I cleared my throat and continued, "He went to jail and I came back here." I finished the last sentence with lot courage.

He looked at me and pain and anger were visible on his face.

"Why you never contacted me? Why? At least you should have called me once!"

"I couldn't. People I loved the most weren't there, so what was the point in calling..."

"Calling someone you never loved, right?" He interrupted.

"It was my battle! My own fight!"

"It's not always your fight alone! It's not always waiting and expecting from those whom we love! Sometimes we need to take a look around at those who love us! Pari, I know you never loved me, but you knew my feeling, didn't you?"

"I..." I murmured.

"But you never once thought of me or anyone who has ever loved you. Did you tell Furqan?" He asked.

"No."

"See!" He slammed, "That's what I am saying. You think only people who would care for you are the ones you love!"

"I do love Furqan!" I protested.

"You do, but not as strongly as you love those who eventually become the reason of your pain. You were hurt by Riz and you left Pakistan. Now you were broken by some people whom you considered as a sister and a brother, so you left Dubai. Why are you playing with your life?"

He looked at me for an answer. I had none.

He continued, "Pari, stop this hide and seek. One frustrated man who tried hurting you has already earned for his crime. He did because he is evil! Stop blaming yourself for that!"

I looked at him with surprise as he was reading my mind. I looked at him and opened my mouth to say something, but tears rolled down my cheek.

"Let's go out. Come!" He stood up.

Amir called the waiter to pay the bill, but he told us a lady who was with us had already paid. I went out with Amir.

"Tell me, now. Tell me everything." He asked kindly.

And I told him everything with sobs and tears. I told him how blessed I felt when I was with Amna, her family and Faiz. How happy I would be even after a long tiring day. He listened to me patiently and once I finished he turned to me, "Pari, what's gone is gone. Your first priority should be your own self. You can't make people stay in your life. You can't make them love you back or love you again. Once they change their mind then nothing in this world can do something. But at least you have a power on yourself. Build your life!"

I listened to him like an obedient child. "I will. That's why I want to go to Canada."

"No, you won't run to a new place, now. Settle down! Give yourself some peace!"

"I will see you tomorrow. Are you free?" I asked him.

"Yes, ma'am!"

I laughed.

He dropped me to the hostel and told me he would pick me next day at 5:00 PM. After long time I felt my shoulders got relieved from some burden. I felt the peace which had been missing and my instincts told me good things were going to happen soon. That night I slept without reflecting about the past. I closed my eyes without wondering if someone would be missing me or not. That was their problem and I was no more concerned if they missed me or not.

Next morning, I got up and laughed because a day before I went to buy some essential stuff and I didn't buy any. I called Tina, "Mummy-to-be, I don't have toothpaste and that's only because you engaged me in international gossips, yesterday." I spoke, as soon as she said hello.

She laughed, "I told you to come at my place, I never run out of toothpaste!"

"I will and then you have to stock all my favourite food as well!" My long-lost amiable soul was back.

"Pari, I noticed something, yesterday."

"What?" I asked causally.

"You love Amir!" she said without any hesitation.

"God! You will never change! You and your assumptions!" I laughed.

"Well, I am not a kid."

"Are you a seer?"

"I don't know what is a seer. Probably a fortune teller, right?"

"Yeah." I smiled.

"Can't you use simple language?"

"Tell me, how do you know that?"

"What?" She pretended.

"You know, what you just said."

She laughed, "Ah! Curious? So you love him!"

"No! I mean..."

"Yes, now think of an excuse. Well, yesterday, when Amir entered, you thought for a moment that I married him, right?"

She was a keen observer, I couldn't help appreciating that. "Yeah, for a second."

"And in that second your face turned pale."

"Really?" I was shocked she noticed that. *Was that so clear?*

"Of course."

"I like him, but…"

"That is even enough. Pari, he loves you."

"I know! But how do you know that? Ah! Musa must have told you. They are best friends."

"He was very disturbed once you left. So we both knew."

I laughed, "Yeah, you must have given him a counselling session."

"Sort of," she laughed, "Well, he looked happy, yesterday. Now don't leave him."

"I've to think about it." I replied honestly. After the call ended I went to the next room with my toothbrush and I knocked at the door. A girl that seemed to be in a hurry opened the door, "Can I have a pinch of toothpaste?" I asked with a grin.

She was surprised at such a sudden request, but promptly said, "Sure". She went inside the bathroom and got me the toothpaste tube. I put a little and gave her back, "Thank you. By the way, I'm Pari."

"Hi, Pari." She didn't tell her name so I left.

She doesn't seem in a good mood. I smiled and wondered if in the past few years I had had the same attitude. *God knows what people would be calling me at my back*, I thought and smiled.

I chose my most favourite long black dress. I ironed it and went to take a shower. My appetite seemed to be lost. I was anxious to see Amir. *I miss him*, I thought. *I shouldn't. No more emotional attachment*, I warned myself.

At 4:00 PM I sat on my bunk with the phone in my hand. I dialled his number several times and every time I cancelled it. I was too scared to think of the future and I had no intention to break once more. I started growing religiously stronger and the connection with God helped me to heal. I was certain that when I was trapped by Jabir he could have done anything, and the delivery boy from the grocery was not a coincidence. It was a miracle. I wanted to take it as a miracle and to believe that nothing would go wrong.This time I decided not to listen to my heart or mind and let God write alone what He thought was best for me. I had learned that my plans were the weakest, and that my hopes and wishes were incomplete, without His will.

I lay down, I put on the ear phones and started deleting the songs which had been my companion during the saddest nights. *Sad Movies Always Make Me Cry* reminded me of days when I encircled myself with memories of Riz and would cry every night. I loved the song, but I had to delete that because the catharsis phase had to end. I had to accept the lesson my mother once taught me.

When I was ten I found an old nest in a brick hole in our house. There were several empty nests, some on the trees and a few in windows. I asked Ama why there weren't any birds in them. She said, "My child, once the birds fly they never return."

"But they made these nests with so much love and effort."

"Once you fly you don't remember the effort it took to make them and now new birds occupy the old nest. This is the law, a universal law."

I understood this law after twenty years.

While I was purging the music list of my phone, it started ringing. It was Amir. I smiled and answered the call, "Such a punctual soul you are," I said cheerfully.

"And I hope you are, too. I am coming in fifteen minutes," he said.

I looked at the clock and it was fifteen to five.

"Yes, I am ready."

"Great then. See you soon."

I got up, brushed my hair and observed myself in the mirror. *I look so pale. I should have got a haircut. Why am I criticizing myself?* I knew I was getting conscious and I hated that feeling.

Ten minutes later Amir called again, "I am outside."

"You are five minutes early," I joked.

"Okay, then come out five minutes later."

I started to laugh. I carried my handbag and went out. He was checking his looks in the view mirror. *So he is conscious, too.* Seeing me he straightened up. I sat down and I could smell the perfume: I couldn't hide my smile. He got nervous and asked, "What happened?"

"Have you just broken a bottle of perfume?" He smiled shyly and looked at the road.

"Where are we going?"

"There's a new restaurant in F10 and after that we will go to my place."

"Your place? Why?" I was surprised.

"My mom is waiting there for us."

I was startled, but I managed to hide my expressions, "So let's go there first."

"No. First I need to ask you something."

I had an idea of what he was trying to say."All right, you can ask here. We don't have to order food for that."

"It won't sound romantic."

I smiled and this time I looked out.

"Well, it doesn't have to be romantic. It has to be true. It has to be sincere." I spoke while looking out.

"Marry me, Pari."

He said it.

"Even knowing I had an affair with Riz?"

"It doesn't matter."

"Even knowing I was almost sexually assaulted?"

"Even then!" He stressed. "I told you that was not your fault. Don't let those things stigmatize you."

"What about your family? Will they accept me?"

"We don't need to tell about our past to everyone. We don't need to show our scars to every person we meet in our lives. Not everyone is a healer."

"And are you?"

"I do not promise to be a magician and heal each of your wounds. But I do promise that I won't peel them. I do promise that I won't give you any aches."

"And love?" I asked like a hungry and tired traveller.

"Of course I love you and will always do."

I smiled and looked straight in his eyes without reading them, "I want to meet your mom."

He smiled and nodded and started to drive.

Twenty-nine

Amir's mother was a humble lady, and unlike other moms she wasn't possessive and showed no objection. My only fear, that she may disapprove that I had no family except Furqan, was gone when I met her.

"I need Amir's happiness. That's you."

I was so grateful to her for such kindness which was usually not found in many mother-in-laws. She didn't ask me once about my family or financial background. I was sure Amir had convinced her brilliantly.

A few days later, we were engaged in an intimate function where only the closest relatives and friends of Amir were invited. Furqan couldn't reach us, as his leave was not approved by his company due to such short notice. I called Sobia and Salma and informed them and expressed my wish for them to be there for me, but they mentioned they were busy with their children and family and told me their blessings were with me. I never called anyone else because I knew the answer. Furqan sent me money for the engagement and I bought a readymade outfit for the event. I bought some artificial jewellery which went perfectly with the dress, though one of Amir's aunts showed her disapproval for I was wearing artificial jewellery rather than gold.

"It's not in our tradition to give artificial jewellery to our daughters."

Amir's mom quickly intervened, "But *MashaAllah* she looks stunning!"

"She does. But what people would say?"

"There are no "people", all are family members."

"But parents should take care of such things."

She was unaware of my situation and when she mentioned them it made me uneasy and emotional. I was sitting quietly with my head bent down like a traditional girl. I looked at Amir's mom.

"She doesn't have parents," she whispered.

"But her mother never left anything of hers to pass on to her daughter?"

She was persistent and didn't show any sign of guilt for how she was hurting my feelings. She had no pity. She was concerned only about ornaments which had nothing to do with her.

The gathering for men and women was separate with no exceptions; therefore Amir was with males, of course. After the dinner was served his sister brought him and he sat with me. Though I had known him for so many years still my heart missed a beat. I couldn't look at him, but kept staring at my hands on my lap. Amir's mother handed over him a ring and he held my hand and quietly put it around my ring finger. Thankfully Furqan had sent me enough money and I bought the ring for Amir. It was a silver ring, although gold is prohibited in Islam for men, still the aunt frowned when she saw the silver ring. I had given the ring to Tina before the function started, and she gave it back to me and I put it on Amir's finger. It fitted perfectly his finger and that made me smile. Amir was surprised to see a ring; probably he wasn't expecting it from me. After the function ended I went to Tina's house and stayed there for the night. It wasn't decent to stay at Amir's place before the marriage.

After the engagement Amir mentioned to me he needed a year of time to get married, I was afraid, but I never showed him my fears. I also thought to get a job so that I could be an independent woman. During that time I got mail from Shaw: he mentioned that some prestigious company was hiring candidates and he asked me to send my documents. He didn't know I already had left Dubai and when I mentioned to him he was disappointed. He asked for my number and I sent him and he called me the same day,

"Hey, Pari! Disappeared like a fairy, right?" He teased me.

"I had no other option."

"I am really sorry for all that happened. At least you should have called me, before going."

"I was so upset that time. Well, I don't want to recall that time."

"I'm sorry. So, what's up?"

"I got engaged and I am looking for work here."

"Wow! Congratulations!" He sounded happy, "When is the wedding?"

"Not now. He has gotten a job, but he needs to settle things. Like saving and all."

"Great, then you can come and work here during that time."

I hesitated for a moment, "I don't know. I don't think so."

"Why not, Pari? You can't give up! You can get lots of opportunities here!"

"I don't know if Amir will agree."

"So his name is Amir!"

I smiled.

"Discuss with him and let me know. But don't give up, Pari!"

"Thank you, Shaw. You are so kind." I promised him that I would definitely discuss the thing with Amir, though I was certain he would not agree. It is quite common in woman's world that their decisions are apparently in their hands, but are only made with concern of their husbands and in-laws. After a few days I met Amir in a restaurant and after listening to his entire week's schedule I told him about Shaw's call. He was mute for more than a minute and reading his mind I said, "It's okay. I understand. I have just told you." I changed the topic, "How is Mum?" After the engagement I had started to call his mother "Mum". I was slowly trying to love each and every person and thing associated with him. I was trying to love him, too.

"I will not stop you from working. You have worked as hard as I have. More than me. I know how hard you struggled to come here, so, I won't let that struggle be wasted."

"Will you convince your parents? Will they approve if I go to Dubai alone?"

"I will come with you. I will find a work there, too."

"What about the job? Your job?"

"I will find a job there."

"You don't have to do that for me!" It gave me guilt to think that he had to take that trouble for me.

"I am not doing that for you but for myself. I can't send you alone."

"I won't go, then," I said firmly.

"No more argument, now. I am starving!" He held the fork and knocked on the table mimicking a judge in a court, "Let's order food."

I frowned to tease him. We ordered the food and moved the conversation to various topics. He drove me back, "Pari, I don't want you to be in a hostel anymore. It's hard to live there."

"Not really. I am used to that."

"You can move to my place."

I laughed."Your aunt would kill you!"

"She is quite nosy, isn't she?" He laughed too.

"Seriously, why don't you move to my place?" He sounded serious.

"Are you crazy? You know how everyone will react!"

"I have a solution to that."

"And what's that?" I looked at him surprised.

"We can have *nikkah.* A small ceremony. We can marry."

I was quite surprised. "Are you sure? You weren't ready..."

"I guess I am now."

I stared at him and asked, "Means?"

"Pari, few things we understand them at their right time, neither before that, nor after it. Do you understand what I mean?"

"I guess I do." I smiled.

"I'll talk to Mom. You apply for the job and we will leave together."

That night I emailed Shaw and sent along my documents. I told him that I would be not coming alone but with Amir. I was not scared anymore, but I was definitely worried how to walk on the same roads where I left so many beautiful memories with Faiz and Amna. And I was afraid of walking on the roads where I had the bitter memories.

Amir convinced his family and we got married within a month. It was not a big marriage. We simply had a paper marriage in presence of a few guests. We never had a honeymoon, as Amir couldn't afford one and we never had much time. We left for Dubai after two weeks of wedding, I on a work permit and Amir on visit visa. After staying a week in a hotel we moved to an apartment and Shaw helped us more than we could imagine. Shaw helped us getting a reasonable accommodation and paid the money saying we could return him later. He helped Amir in seeking the job too. So we started our life: a journey of a lifetime.

Thirty

I was married to Amir for 25 years. I started this journal ten years ago, but I couldn't pen down everything. Now I feel that the time has come to complete this incomplete story. Amir and I never had kids and, though we were told by friends and family several times to adopt a baby, I never agreed. Amir never let the feeling of emptiness overcome me. He kept me busy in his love. He made me a strong person which my parents couldn't. He taught me that to love oneself is as important as loving another person. I do not say I had a fairytale life like I would imagine in my 20s. Our life was filled with struggle from the nadir and faced the obstacles which are faced by every starter. There were times we found our boat sinking in little complaints and misunderstandings. But eventually we would forget everything and fall in love all over again. Marriage isn't a fairy tale: it's a reality which needs to be made a fairy tale through patience. It has to be masqueraded at times, too. Masquerade helps the marriage from getting crowded when the days are blue. It saves from seeking advice from the wrong person. It's not bad to play the masquerade, as once you get the things settled, the real love comes back.

I would often miss many people from my past. I missed having loving parents and the joy which is gotten from the care and concern of them. I never forgot Ama and would sometimes look at her photo and cry, but Amir used to soothe me that I will meet her in heaven. I believed him every time. I never once thought of Rizwan or Jabir. I decided to move on without waiting to see karma knocking them down. People often say that those who hurt us, first pay back, then they come back and apologize. Well, that's not completely true. They might pay back for what they do to us, but they never get the courage to apologize. Neither Rizwan nor Jabir ever apologized and I didn't wait for any revenge.

Jabir once mailed me and it just said, *Stay always happy.* I wonder what the purpose was. He didn't say he was sorry. I don't know if Jabir or Riz ever felt sorry or not, but I had forgiven them long ago. People who were mutual friends of Riz often mentioned that he got married and had a happy life. He had a daughter and he was an over-protective father. After his daughter's marriage he discovered the husband had an extramarital affair and the girl committed suicide. Riz totally broke and stopped meeting anyone from his family and friends. When I got the news I was saddened. The girl suffered for what her father did many years ago. Karma has no deadline and it comes when we have already forgotten our pain.

We moved back to Pakistan and here I spend most of my time in orphanage with the stars that lost the sky. I miss Faiz sometimes and wish we had more of our time. He never contacted and never tried to reach me. I never deleted him from my social site, so I knew few of the things happened in his life. He is a professional pilot and when I saw the photo of his first solo flight, I made his favourite dark chocolate cake and celebrated with Amir. While cutting the cake I hugged Amir and cried in his arms like a baby. Yes, after Ama, he is the one whose memories make me cry. I don't know if he got married or not as he is never active on any social media. When years ago I met Faiz, I never knew it would turn into our last meeting.

With each passing day I learnt that a person's best friend can be a spouse. The closest one in one's own self. But the truest friend who knows every single thing about us is God. He never leaves. He never needs to be told what went wrong. I am not well and I know the time has come to meet Ama and Amir in heaven. One thing which broke my heart is the thought that I would be laid alone in the grave till the Day of Judgment. I smile, sometimes, when I think about those days when I wished to send the news of my departure to the people I loved the most. I wanted to see all those faces around me, but I think when death approaches we want to be alone. We don't want spectators. Death slowly takes away all the wishes and love before taking our soul away. We want it to end soon and get rid of this pain as if someone is peeling the soul from body.

I don't know if this diary would ever be read or not, I wish God gives me one chance to somehow be back and peek for a moment. This journal was not for Amir, because we had our times together. He knew how much he was loved by me and I know how much he loved me back. This diary is for Faiz. Who came in my life as a brother and left as a son. He lived inside me all these years though I never carried him in my womb. I never understood why I loved him with this intensity, but I think God wanted me to experience little moments of being a mother as he knew I would never be one. If you are reading this, Faiz, then remember you had two mothers. One who came just for a short time: she was just eight years older than you, but she loved you silently all these years. If there's someone you ever loved and couldn't tell, then go and tell them. Untold love is no less than agony.

FAIZ

Thirty-one

I am looking at all the blank pages of this thick journal. It's 6:00 AM and I want to open the door of each room *where is she*? Where is my *Baaji, Baaji* who was my mother. I was never good at expressing, but she should know I loved her like a son loves his mom. But where is she? Why Hoor didn't mention any of Amir's death last night? I go downstairs and look around to see *Baaji.* She must have woken up by now or may be Amir is around. I see Shafi Baba in the kitchen making tea, "*Salam*, Shafi Baba."

"*Walikum Salam*, you got up early?" He smiles softly.

"Actually I didn't sleep. Where are *Baaji* and her husband Amir?"

The smile disappears from Shafi Baba's face.

"I will call Hoor. You go and sit in dining hall. Hoor said she will make you breakfast."

Why is he avoiding my questions? I start getting panic. Shafi Baba goes inside and I start looking at walls. There is only one wall with photos: I can recognize Pari *Baaji* as a child and then there are some photographs of a boy. This probably is her husband as the colours of the photo are faded. I see the photo of *Baaji* and her husband as a newlywed couple and then the series of photos of her journey with Amir. I hear Hoor's voice at my back who is saying something to Shafi Baba. Then she calls me, "Amir, what would you have for a breakfast?"

"Where is *Baaji*?" I ask like the same old stubborn boy.

"Why don't you have breakfast first and then we can talk?"

"I don't want to eat anything. Tell me what's going on?"

"Have you read the diary?"

"I have."

"I don't know what is in it, as she never gave us the permission to read it."

Gave? I am shocked, why she used the past tense?

"Where is she?" I lose the cool.

"Wait a moment," she says and disappears inside the room.

She comes with an envelope in her hand. She sits in front of me and places the envelope in her lap.

"Faiz, your *Baaji* has passed away two weeks ago."

"What!!! Why you never mentioned that before?!" I stand up.

"I will tell you everything. Listen. Sit, please."

I sit down unwillingly. "Tell me. Please." I am in tears.

"I am Furqan's daughter, her brother, as you know. My father died a year ago. I was born in Canada and still live there. A month ago Aunt called me just after the death of Amir Uncle. They both seemed so much in love that Aunt couldn't bear his death."

She looks at me and waits for me to say something, but I have no words. She continues,

"When I came here she looked quite ill and refused to see any doctor.

She said she had had her time and there's nothing that could be done. She handed me that box I gave you last night and your contact number. She didn't tell me much about her relation with you, but she said 'he is my lost son'. She asked me to message you only after her death and must not give you the news of her death. She had had her own reasons, which even I don't know. Along with the box she gave me this letter and asked me to read it only if you would come."

"What if I hadn't come?" I interrupt.

"She said 'if after giving the message to Faiz that his *Baaji* wants to see him and he doesn't show up, then the letter, along with the box, must be destroyed'."

I am unable to understand why she didn't ask to see me when she had my contact. I put both hands on my face. I am utterly blank.

"Shall I read the letter?" Hoor asks.

I nod.

She tears the envelope from one side and takes out a white paper. She unfolds the letter and starts to read,

Dear Faiz,

I am glad you are here. You came all the way to see me. I understand how disappointed you must be to find out that I am no longer in this world. When I gave that box to Hoor she insisted that I should see you before I go. She couldn't understand the logic behind this act. I am sure you need an answer too. My child, now you already have known the events which occurred and composed my life. I expected a lot from people when I shouldn't have. After marrying to Amir my life started to change. I started to grow and to become stronger than I could have ever imagined. He never let me change in love. He gave me my own space and I grew without bending. I sometimes would talk about you with Amir, but then he would persuade me to focus on things I got in life rather than on what I lost. I never adopted a child, but I run my shelter home and that's where I have given our possessions. Amir and I together made this house, so I don't want it to be demolished so I have given this to the orphanage. Now this quiet calm house will echo with the sounds of children's footsteps, their crackles and cries. I might see that from the sky, I hope. I don't have much to give to Hoor, so I have left the money in my account to her. For you I do not wish to leave something mortal, so I am passing you my memories and love.

Now, coming back to why I never called you while I was alive. Faiz, no matter how old I am and how much strong I have been, I still have a fear. I have a fear of breaking up the hope I carried all these years. A hope, that Faiz loved me as a brother and a son. When my mother died I saw all the people come to her funeral whom I never met. I didn't see those whom my mother kept calling till her last breath, but they never came, saying they were too busy. I always had that feeling that she never died of a heart attack, but of a broken heart. Her hopes were gone so she left the world. I want to leave joyfully because Amir waits for me. I do not wish to see you never coming when I am in this world. Just remember I left happily on a belief that somewhere you still miss me and think of me.

And now the second reason why I asked Hoor not to break the news of my death earlier. Faiz, many people rush to see us when we are no longer breathing. When our body is too cold to feel the warmth of their touch and we can no longer smell their fragrance. But it hardly happens when we get the calls during our lives, when we receive the flowers in our hands than on our graves. If Hoor had told you about my death, then I am sure you would have rushed here, but that doesn't make a difference. The difference would be when you come here unaware of my death. When you come here to see a woman who loved you enormously twenty-five years ago. If you are here, then let me give you all the love I couldn't give you in the past years. Faiz, I left and never returned because I never wanted to hate you. I left with some love in my heart and I hope some in yours too. I hope you have a family who loves you a lot. Go and tell them you love them too. Go and find some Faiz who isn't part of your family to share some love with. Faiz, this life is too short to do all the things we ever wish to do and one of the most important wishes, which is often left unfulfilled, is the wish to know we are loved! And we can only know that if we are generous enough to give it.

You shall always be loved.

Yours Baaji.

Hoor starts crying and so do I. We keep sitting in the same position. I, captain Faiz, have always carried the anger and the ego I inherited from my dad. Today I carry something which isn't passed to me through my blood, but a care and a love that kept protecting me all these years.

I take my trolley bag and carry the presents and the box in my hand. Before leaving I ask Shafi Baba to take me to the cemetery. He calls a cab and then I head towards the cemetery. I reach there and Shafi Baba shows me two plain graves with no tombstone on them.

"Why there are no names?"

"It was their will. The first one is of Amir and the one next to the tree is

Pari's."

She didn't want to leave behind her name, but just love.

"Baba, please, wait here." I request Shafi baba.

"*Acha, beta.* Okay, Son."

I reach to the Amir's grave, "Thank you, Amir, for keeping my *Baaji* happy. For giving her all the love and happiness that she deserved."

I walk further and sit by Pari's grave.

"No epitaph? No signs? I know you are in peace. You are more than happy there so you don't need any words above you. Your Faiz is here. Your son and brother! You were never childless. You were always in my heart, but my heart was too stoned to break the ego. Thank you for giving me all this love. I wish you would have taken a little risk of calling me before, going. Well, no complaints. I understand. I am going, but I promise you that I will light someone's world like you did for me. I brought these books for you, but I will give them to someone whom I pass your love. I hope I will not be hurt, at the end, because I am not strong like you."

I walk out of the cemetery, sit in the car and head towards the airport.

ACKNOWLEDGEMENTS

No story is completed without characters and no task is done without the support and help of kind friends. I owe my gratitude to many people who stood by me all this time. It's my editor Daniele, who didn't only edit my novel, but gave me his feedback on each character and scene. Thank you, Daniele.

Also, I'm thankful to Dastan team for helping me publish this book in Pakistan.

My utmost thanks to my colleagues and friends from all over the world. Thank you Hiba Abdullah, Maima Faisal, Kinza Malik, Alfa Holden, Christina Strigas, Aqsa, Komal Malik, Amina, Abrar, Nishtha, Uzma, Darshan, Waqas, Saurabh, Mr. Chandra and so many more. You people made me continue when I lost my energy.

A very special thanks to my readers and Instagram's followers. Without you people this wouldn't be possible.

And finally, thank you, Adnan. You are a dream which even angels wish to come true. I love you to the sky and beyond.

GLOSSARY

Ama Mother

Aba Father

AED Arab Emarati Dirham

Baaji A term used for older sister or woman

Beti Daughter

Beta Son

Halwa Dessert

InshaAllah If Allah wills

Jee Yes

MashaAllah God has willed

Mabrook Congratulation

Murree A town in Pakistan

Mehr A mandatory payment promised to pay by groom to bride at the time of marriage.

Namaz-e-janaza Funeral Prayer

Sahib Sir

Shalwar Kameez Pakistani dress

Sadar A market in Rawalpindi

You can find more of author's work on:
www.humadnan.com
Instagram:
@athousandyearsoflearning
Facebook:

A Thousand Years of Learning